o Moved My Share Price?

Who Moved My Share Price?

A business parable for 21st Century Management

ANDY ANDREWS

TED BLACK

JONATHAN BALL PUBLISHERS
JOHANNESBURG & CAPE TOWN

ISBN 1 86842 130 9

Published in 2002 by
JONATHAN BALL PUBLISHERS (PTY) LTD
PO Box 33977
Jeppestown 2043

Reprinted 2002

Cover design, typesetting and reproduction by
Triple M Design & Advertising, Johannesburg
Printed and bound by CTP Book Printers,
Caxton Street, Parow, Cape
15373

Contents

Introduction

You will enjoy this story. Based on true events, it shows why so many global marquee companies have fallen off the leader board recently. Their strategic blunders have been disastrously costly.

There are several reasons for their fall from grace, but three are critical:

Firstly, in every business failure of the last 20 years anywhere in the world, you will find that the board of directors was the last to realise that things were going badly wrong.

Secondly, managers do not know that their *only* legitimate purpose is to *maximise the value of the firm* for shareholders.

Thirdly, they are unaware that value derives fundamentally from sustainable productivity of the firm's asset base, not the productivity of its people.

That may surprise you if you believe in the 'common sense' of controlling costs and planning for profit growth.

But if you use the **ROAM** model explained in

this story (Return on Assets Managed), you will understand why asset productivity is the true measure of operating management's competence, and you won't make that fundamental mistake. Managers make a 'Return on Assets'. Shareholders, 'owners', make a 'Return on Investment'.

Using the ROAM model means educating people from boardroom to task level with numbers – the ROAM numbers, and one in particular: **ATO** (Asset Turnover), or *asset spin* as we call it.

Giving people the ROAM numbers creates the conditions for people to think like owners – to see the big picture and develop the confidence to challenge and change the way you compete.

You will understand how one person's actions affect others; how each department depends on the rest; what impact individuals have on the entire company. It shows you how to make money and generate cash playing the game of business.

Moreover, once you use and understand the ROAM model, you will get to grips with finance – a prerequisite if you want to be a first-class manager. To be first-class, you have to be ROAM-focussed.

So, at the end of the book, pick up your calculator and do as Simon says and did.

Strike off in a new direction and spin your

assets. You'll be in for a great game and a thrilling one at that!

Andy Andrews & Ted Black
Johannesburg, 2002

NOTE:

This story is based on actual events.

Names have been changed to protect the innocent and the guilty.

No women are in the cast of characters. Men lost this plot.

PROLOGUE:

Simon rakes the coal

James Cole, founder of Measurement Data Systems (MDS), stands at his office window and gazes over a rolling, manicured lawn. The early morning dew and sunlight turn it into a sparkling, emerald setting for the company's office buildings that ring it.

He feels good. It's his first day back at work after a week away at one of the finest golf courses in the world. Like many marquee companies today, his firm sponsors an annual golf tournament.

The occasion was a celebration to crown a triumphal year. During it, MDS grew in leaps and bounds. Listed on several international Stock Exchanges, it is high up the ranks of the biggest companies in its market sector.

Capitalising on the worldwide IT and e-commerce revolution, his company has won global recognition. He can be proud of his achievements since starting MDS 20 years ago.

Turning to his desk, he glances at the mail and picks up a letter with a CV attached to it. He thinks, 'What the hell is this? Why hasn't it gone to someone in HR?'

Then a chart catches his eye. It sparks his interest and he starts reading. The writer is a college student. It turns out he is also a shareholder, albeit a very minor one, with a provocative point of view.

> 31 January 01
>
> Dear Mr Cole
>
> I am writing to you for two reasons. First, I am lucky enough to own a few MDS shares, 100 actually. They have done well for me so far. Second, I am in the final year of a degree but would like to start my work career now.
>
> On the first count, as an 'owner' so to speak, I wish to test some thoughts. I don't fully understand what shareholder value is all about or what may happen to the share price.
>
> To help ask some of my questions, I used a productivity model called ROAM. I am told that few companies or managers know about it. Apparently, even fewer use it, and that includes accountants.
>
> The critical number in the model appears to be Asset Turnover (ATO, which is Sales ÷ Assets).
>
> Based on data from firms all over the

world[1], the chart below shows clearly the relationship between ATO and ROAM.

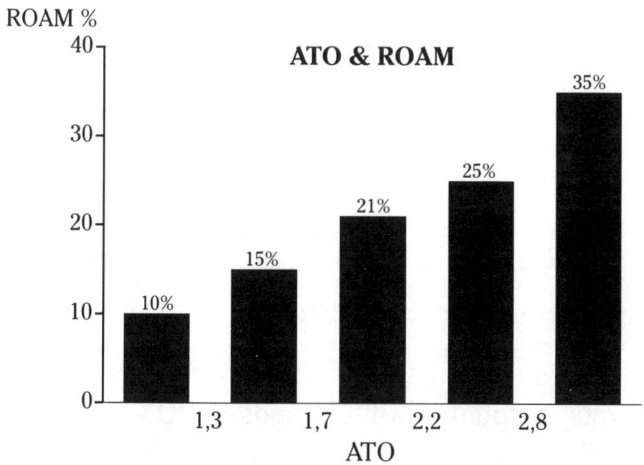

When ATO rises, so does the chance of a higher return on total assets.

MDS results fit the research perfectly but place it at the low end of the curve. This troubles me so I have done a very simple productivity analysis.

I converted numbers taken from your annual reports into some other charts. The first is Return on Sales % (ROS, which is Operating Profit ÷ Sales x 100). As you can see, the trend since 1991 is not good at all.

Has competition caused this fall? Maybe costs and expenses grew faster

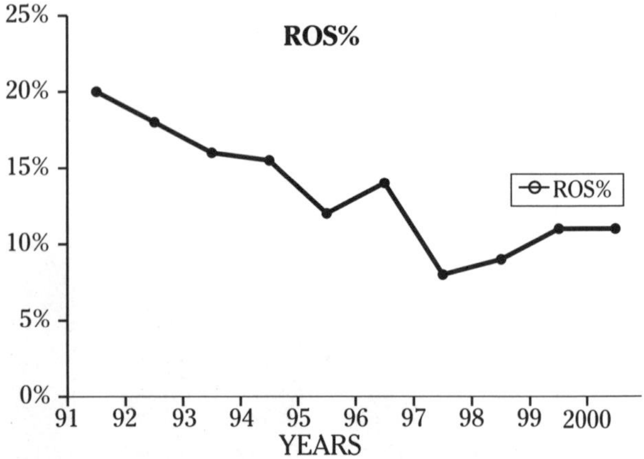

than sales. It's hard to find reasons in your accounts, but I suppose a 10% ROS is still quite good. Is it OK for your industry?

Next is the sales productivity of the asset base - your Asset Turnover (ATO) for the last four years.

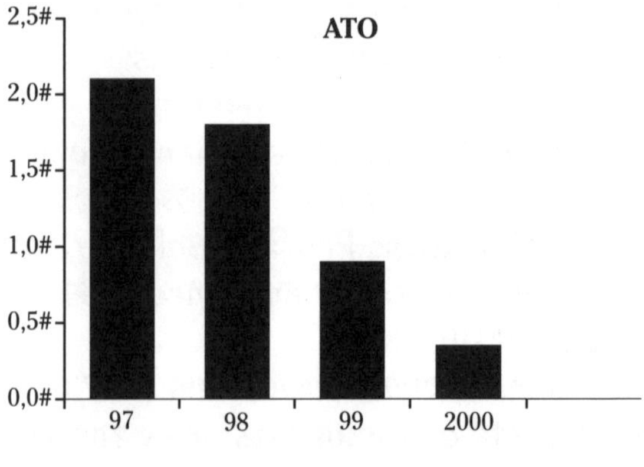

Assets grew 31 times in four years - sales 5 times. This is huge growth but due mainly to buying new companies and paying a lot of 'goodwill' for them - whatever that means. It is why your ATO slowed down sharply from 2,1 to 0,3.

You have lots of cash in the bank. I suppose you collected most of that from your latest Stock Exchange listing. It also seems you mainly use MDS shares to buy companies. Is the cash there to support the shares, or are you going to buy more businesses with it?

The amortisation story confuses me too. If you buy a company, it costs you money. For an owner, it's cash spent and you want a return for it. How can you 'amortise' it - write it off - as accountants say you have to do? Isn't it fair to expect a return on the original amount you paid?

The ATO slow-down isn't due just to growth. Customers take longer to pay - 60 days in 1995 and 120 days today. Stock also turns over much more slowly than it used to do.

The next graph tells the whole story. ROAM started its plunge five years ago

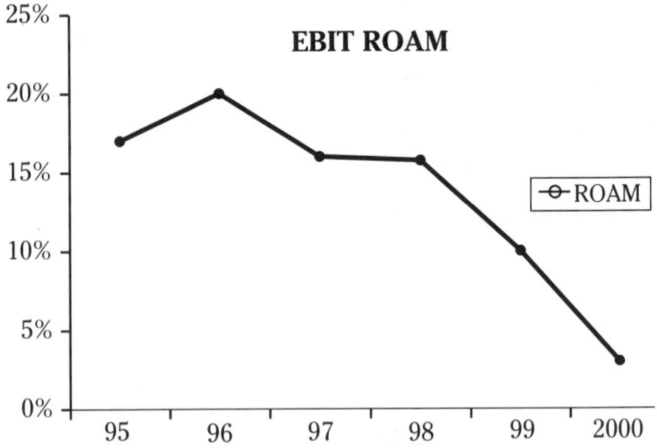

because of your strategy.

MDS's market value was $10 billion at year-end. That's five times bigger than sales revenue of $2 billion, and 50 times bigger than operating profit of $200 million. What drives the share value? It can't be high productivity, can it?

I know I may have the wrong end of the stick, but these charts warn that you will hit a brick wall sooner or later. Shouldn't shareholders be worried? I wonder what ROAM was, say 10 years ago?

I would really appreciate the chance to learn about all this, but more importantly, as an employee. Despite my questions, MDS seems to be a very exciting company. Is there an opportunity for me? I enclose my CV in the hope that you think it worthwhile for someone to see me.

Yours sincerely
Simon Raikes

Cole puts the letter down and thinks, 'Who is this guy?' That's the gist of his thoughts, anyway, because the words he has in mind are not printable. Incensed, he gets up and walks through an adjoining door into his financial director's office. Max Ford is at his desk. Cole drops the letter in front of him and asks, 'Who's this cheeky sod and what the hell is he talking about?'

Max glances through it and says, 'His name doesn't ring a bell.'

'What does this ROAM and ATO stuff mean to us? Has anyone else raised these issues before?'

'He's using "old economy" measures. They don't apply to us,' Max says dismissively.

'Are you sure?'

'Absolutely. Look at the reviews we get from market analysts and merchant bankers. They never refer to "return on assets" – just sales and profit growth.'

'What do we do, then?'

'Ignore him and he'll go away. He's only a student looking for a job. If he pops up again we'll think of something to say. No one will take him seriously.'

With that, Cole turns on his heels and goes back to his office. He has more pressing and urgent matters – like, for instance, another company takeover. More exciting still, he has a new head office to build with a 'corporate university' campus that befits a global, high-tech, 21st-century company. Besides, these diversions allow his mind to suppress the nagging, fundamental concerns the letter raises.

SIMON SAYS:

1. *'All roads lead to ROAM ... or ruin!'*

The story begins at the start of the new millennium and a new academic year. One afternoon, when the birds go tweet tweet, the grass is green and the trees turn slightly golden, our young hero Simon, a diamond loved by one and all, is on a golf practice tee.

He has a fine swing and wields his club like a wand. The balls he hits soar into the blue sky, ending in a tight cluster more than 250 yards down the fairway. It seems magical to those of us less skilled.

By and by, his Dad joins him. He admires his son's shot-making for a while, then suggests, 'What about a quick nine holes before sunset? With few people around and about we have the course to ourselves and can finish easily before dark.'

Simon eagerly agrees because it gives him the chance to raise an idea he has. It concerns his slow progress with a degree and how this tests his ever-loving Dad's patience more than somewhat.

After he hits a huge drive down the middle of the fairway, Simon says as they leave the first tee, 'It is time to find a job while I finish my studies. Student part-time work does not pay well, and I'd like to gain some financial independence instead of relying on you.'

The words please his father no end. 'Well, well, well,' he says, 'this news is good because we face tough times and I have to pull you out of your full-time course at college. However, you must realise that it's hard to hold down a job and study. It will be difficult for you. Also, maybe the time has come to put one of your talents to better use.'

'What are you talking about?'

'You play golf well.'

'So what?'

'This game allows you to rub shoulders with influential business people and to spend five or more uninterrupted hours with them. All you need is your low handicap, a degree, and sales ability, and many opportunities can come your way.'

Simon smiles and says, 'At least I have the low handicap. Now I must finish the degree and learn to sell.'

'That's it, and where are you thinking of looking for work?'

'Everyone is talking about "e-business" and "new economy" companies. The one on people's lips today is Measurement Data Systems, MDS. I'd like to join them,' Simon says.

'Very good thinking. MDS is well respected by all creditable and prominent citizens in this city. What is more, your godmother Louise even bought you some of their stock for your twenty-first birthday. You are a shareholder. They should treat you with respect.'

'With 100 shares? I doubt it. Anyway, how do I get in?'

'Do you know a party there to help introduce you? I don't.'

'Neither do I. Maybe I should contact their human resources department.'

'Forget it. They have "big hat, no cattle". At best, they'll tell you to get qualified first. Aim high instead. Turn this opportunity into a project to raise the heart rate.'

'What do you mean?'

'Go for the top … see the executive chairman, Mr Cole.'

Simon sighs and says, 'You've lost the plot, Dad. These are cool dudes and millionaires many times over. Early this week they flew their private jets to a resort where they sponsor a major pro-am golf tournament. As we speak, they are having a great time on the course and in the casino where they slap backs and do deals with everyone who matters in this city. Cole will never see me.'

'Perfect … he's a keen golfer, too,' his Dad

murmurs thoughtfully. 'All you have to do is grab his undivided attention.'

'How? Which chief executive will take notice of a student seeking a first job? Come on, be realistic.'

Simon is not impressed. Now he is sure his old man has lost it. Then, because he goes quiet, he takes a peek at him and sees a faraway look on his face. It might be a daydream, but often it means he has a stratagem in mind.

Sure enough, he mutters, 'Simon, you own stock. If anyone can focus their minds it has to be an investor – even a small one.'

'Come on, Dad! MDS is worth billions, and listed on several bourses around the world. This is a big company. I have only a few shares. What can we possibly know that they don't? Why would Cole listen to me?'

'Because your letter will rivet him. More than that, even if you don't get a job with them, this little project can turn into a most valuable experience. You will learn more about management and some basic rules of business than you have at college in the last few years. You may not get a job with them, but you'll learn a lot.'

'Thanks very much, but I want to *earn* right now! Maybe I'd do better joining the formal way.'

'Possibly, but you have to admit this is a different approach.'

'Well, I guess I have nothing to lose but a job I don't have anyway. So how do we go about this?' Simon won't admit it, but he is now more than a little curious.

'We'll open their eyes with a DAZZGOTO!'

'A *what?*'

'A *"dazzling glimpse of the obvious"*. There's an old adage, Simon. It says: "In the land of the blind, the one-eyed man is king!"'

'Are you saying these guys are blind and I'm to be the one-eyed king?'

'Blind and maybe a few other things besides. I think their success dazzles many other admirers and punters round and about too. So yes, you are a good one to test them. The last person they expect to do that is a student, even if he is a shareholder.'

'The problem is I struggle with accounts and audit stuff, let alone what it means to be a shareholder.'

'Don't worry about bookkeeping. Leave that to accountants. We are talking *finance*, the bedrock of management. Unless you understand finance, you will never be a first-class manager – only second-class. If you get your mind around a simple financial model called ROAM, you can be first-class. You'll talk confidently with anyone, anywhere, at any level, and be able to ask tough questions.'

'That's some claim you make. So, "All roads lead to ROAM!" Is that it?' Simon asks.

'Absolutely.'

'And it'll teach me the basics of finance.'

'Enough to be an effective manager. You'll use it to confront and test MDS. They could be flying a bit high for their own good. Maybe you can bring them down to earth before it's too late.'

'You mean, all roads lead to ROAM...or ruin!'

They both laugh then Simon asks, 'But what does ROAM mean?'

'It stands for *Return-on-Assets-Managed*, and all you need to assess MDS is their last five annual reports, a calculator, and knowledge of Standard Five Arithmetic!'

'Is that all?'

'That's all. It's like the basics of a good golf swing. You start with your grip and stance. It's the same with business. ROAM tells you how well you apply the basic rules of business.'

Simon thinks about that as he stops to play his second shot. His long drive leaves him a short wedge to the flagstick. He stands behind the ball for a moment to pick his line. The hole is tucked away in the top left-hand corner of the green. A sand bunker guards it and will punish any shot falling short. He steps up to the ball to finesse it softly onto the putting surface, but fluffs it straight into the sand trap instead.

'I don't believe it,' he groans. 'What did I do wrong?'

'I don't know. I wasn't watching closely, but I expect you ignored a golf fundamental, and a business one at that. Drives are only 20% of the game. But if you practise them 80% of the time instead of your short game 80% of the time, it can be fatal.'

'Thanks. That helps a lot,' Simon says irritably. The next shot he has to play is a very difficult one indeed if he is to finish the hole in par.

'Don't mention it. You'll see what I mean when we apply the ROAM model tomorrow,' his Dad says as he walks off to play his next shot.

He leaves Simon looking ruefully at his ball plugged deep in the soft sand close to the lip of the bunker and wondering how he got himself into such a mess.

2. *'Think like an* owner!'

The next day, Simon's Dad says to him, 'Keep one thought uppermost: you are a shareholder and in a strong position when you talk to them.'

'How come?'

'You own a tiny chunk of MDS, and that puts you in the shoes of a shareholder. Think like one. Few managers do.'

'Why is it so important to think that way?'

'Because *management has only one legitimate purpose – to maximise the Value-of-the-Firm for shareholders.'*

'Hang on. Isn't there more to it than that? People talk a lot today about corporate governance and all "stakeholders" – customers, the public, employees, suppliers and the wider community. There's all this concern about the environment too.'

'Corporate governance is a hot issue. However, to put it simply, governments take charge of civic matters like health, education, justice and security. Charities do good works. A business exists only to make money and generate cash by supplying products and services to its customers. If it does that better and at lower cost than any of its competitors, it becomes a smooth-running, cash-compounding machine. That's its sole purpose.'

'So it's all about making money and generating cash,' Simon says.

'Exactly, but that's not to say people, ethics and social responsibility to the wide community do not count. They do, because they fuel the business machine over the long haul and determine its long-term survival. Making asbestos or animal fur products and destroying the planet are all bad news. Treating people as consumables is also bad news. Management's task is to create the conditions for people to grow and make all resources productive. If they don't, there will never be enough money to reward the owners for backing the business with their cash. No firm survives that shortage for long. It's the lifeblood of a business.'

'So managers have to think like owners,' Simon says. 'Is that my angle with these guys? Are you saying they haven't been thinking that way? Maybe putting their interests ahead of shareholders?'

'You be the judge of that. What is MDS's value today? Multiply the share price by the number of shares issued and see what that tells us.'

Simon opens the newspaper to find the stock exchange results. 'The share price was $9,20 yesterday.'

'OK. How many shares are in issue?'

Simon looks at the last annual report and says, 'There are more than a billion shares. That means the value-of-the-firm is around $10 billion. It's a big company.'

'Yes, considering how a bunch of school friends started up the business only 20 years ago, it's a great success story.'

'Why would they listen to me?' Simon asks.

'Your ROAM analysis will grab their attention.'

'Why?'

'Because *fundamentally, the VOF depends on the productivity of its asset base – ROAM – not the men and women who do the work.*'

'I don't understand. Everyone says that business is all about people and that they are the most valuable assets of all – especially today, with all the focus on brains and ideas. "New economy" companies and "intellectual capital" are the latest jargon.'

'That's what they say, but their actions speak louder. It should be about people first, then numbers. It rarely happens. Most managers put the *numbers* cart before the *people* horse. In golf, you use numbers to keep score and keep you honest. It's the same with a business. Numbers tell you how well you play the game. The game of business is all about relationships and growing people, and the currency you use is the product or service you create and sell. However, we'll get to that side of it later. OK?'

'Yes,' says Simon.

'Right, here's the model. Let's go through it, then you use it to analyse MDS.'

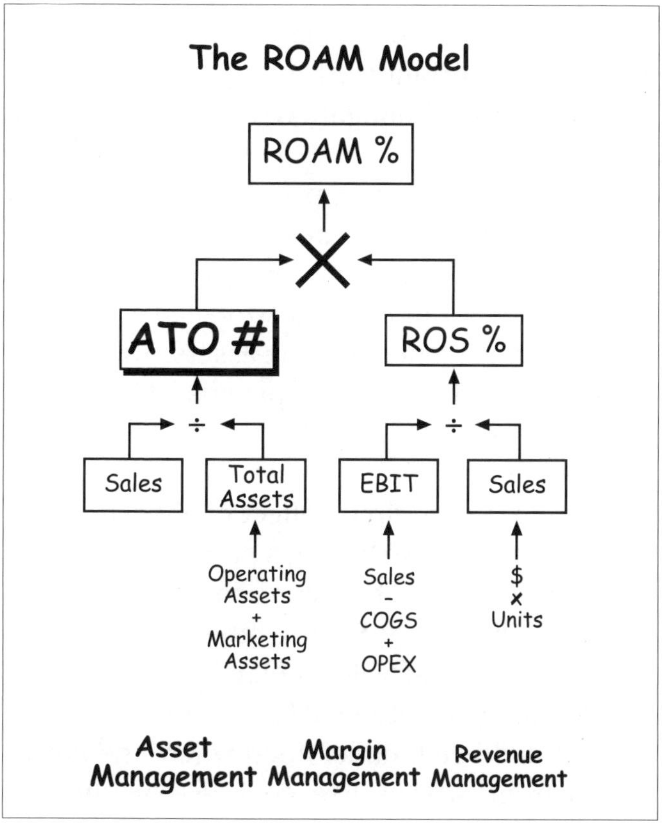

'It shows the dynamic interrelationship between two prime cash flows in the firm:

1. The **Asset** stream on the left (Asset Turnover – **ATO** #).
2. The **Cost/Expense** stream on the right (Return-on-Sales – **ROS%**).

'Multiply the two and you get the **ROAM%**. The three most important measures of operating managers are **ATO** (asset management), **ROS** (margin and revenue management), and **ROAM**. The most important is ATO.'

Simon says, 'I thought ATO was just an "efficiency" measure.'

'That's because few people understand its importance or what it means. Most often, they calculate ROAM by measuring EBIT (Earnings before Interest and Tax, also called Operating Profit) as a percentage of the assets. You get the same answer but it's a myopic way of looking at the business.'

'Why?'

'Leaving the multiplier effect of ATO out of the ROAM picture is like having a patch over one eye and then putting a telescope to it. Or let's use another golf analogy. Sit on a table with your feet off the ground and swing a club.'

'What are you getting at?'

'Do it and you'll understand where the power comes from. ATO is like your legs in the golf swing. They give you huge leverage if you use them properly. ATO does the same for a business.'

'How?'

'There are many reasons. We'll look at some of them.'

'What exactly does ATO measure?'

'The sales productivity of the asset base. It asks: *For each $ of assets, how many $s of sales do we generate?'*

He continues, 'In other words, it asks how many times a year do we "turn", or "use', the assets. $1 of sales from $1 of assets is one "turn". $2 of sales from $1 of assets is two "turns". The aim is to squeeze more sales out of each $ of assets – to "turn" them over more and more often.'

'What are the assets?'

'The "tangible" assets in the balance sheet. They don't include people who come in as costs and expenses on the ROS side of the model. Nor do they include "intangible" things like the value put on patents or "goodwill". For pure ROAM, look at the balance sheet and add up all the tangible ones – land, buildings, plant, inventory, accounts receivable (also called "debtors"), and cash in the bank. We call them "operating" and "marketing" assets in the model.'

'Why?'

'To show that flesh-and-blood *people* make them productive – especially men and women at grass roots in "line" functions like production, marketing and sales. They manage assets at the front line day-to-day.'

He continues, 'Managers talk a lot about profit margins. Always check which one they mean. The "bottom-line" margin for operating managers is EBIT ROS – the profit margin on sales before interest and tax. It answers the second marketing question: *For every $ of sales revenue how many cents profit do we make?*'

'With these two key questions you'll test if MDS understands that the value of the company ultimately depends on asset productivity – especially its sales productivity of assets. Many managers blindly accept the "common-sense" of cost control and plan for growth of sales and profit in isolation. They miss this point completely, and MDS has sure done that. Costs, margins and profits only mean something when you *compare them to sales*. However, that is less than half the story.'

'So you're saying Cole and his people do not have the "big picture"?'

'Yes, I am.'

'So, what must I do now?'

'Mark a ROAM scorecard for them because they aren't doing that. Take these annual reports and pull out three numbers as far back as you can go – the assets, the sales and the EBIT. Do the ATO, ROS and ROAM calculations, then we'll talk again.'

'Suddenly this is getting very interesting,' Simon admits.

As he makes for his room with the annual reports, the ROAM model and a calculator, he says to himself, 'So that's it. Think like an owner if you want to see the big picture.'

3. *'ATO makes, or breaks, your ROAM!'*

Simon yells after an hour or so, 'Dad! I've finished.'

'Coming,' his father calls back from the garden where he is hitting golf balls into a net. As he walks into the house he says, 'A great golf swing and a great business have one thing in common.'

'What?'

'Balance. It's all about balance. Finish every shot in balance, facing your target, elbows in front, weight on the left side and up on your right toe. Do that and you have swung well. Picture any top player – always in perfect balance at the finish of the swing from driver down to putter. The head barely moves and if it does, it moves back to stay behind the ball giving you power and balance. The hands and arms work together, and so do the legs and feet. They're all in harmony – one smooth flow from start to finish. It's the same for a business. Balance is the key to winning the game.'

When he sees Simon shaking his head at him he laughs and says, 'You don't make the connection, do you? You will. Show me what you've done.'

Simon pulls out his workings and they look at the numbers together.

'What do they tell us?'

'I have sales and EBIT numbers for ten years. ROS has fallen from 20 to 10% – even lower in some years.'

'What causes that, do you think?'

'Maybe there's more competition today.'

'What're the effects?'

'You get price-cutting and maybe they have not controlled costs so well because of their big growth. For example, to run a major golf tournament and build a new head office costs plenty.'

'Those are all good points, especially the big growth. It's like doubling your weight in a year. Your system can't handle it. Neither can a company. What about the ATO?'

'Less than one "turn" in a year. In 1997, they generated $2,10 for a $ of assets. Today, they generate 80 cents. Their ATO has slowed down sharply from 2,1 to 0,8, and ROAM tumbled from 18% to 8%,' Simon says.

'Fascinating ... what else?'

'They have a lot of cash in the bank, $1,7 billion. More than that, they have more than $3 billion of "intangible" assets. They call it "goodwill"– it's for companies they bought. You said it shouldn't be part of the calculation, but it's there. What do we do about it?'

'That's another good question. Let us handle that one when you compose a letter to the chairman. First, though … all that cash … where does it comes from?'

'They listed their international operations last year. That big event raised most of it. The rest comes from doing business. I wonder what they intend doing with it.'

'Ask them. Meanwhile, go back to the ATO law. Look at this chart. What does it tell us?'

'As ATO rises so does ROAM,' Simon says.

'Correct. It isn't a guarantee, but highly probable. Data from thousands of companies all over the world tell us that those with a low ATO are much less profitable than those with a high one. Depending on your business, you only start to

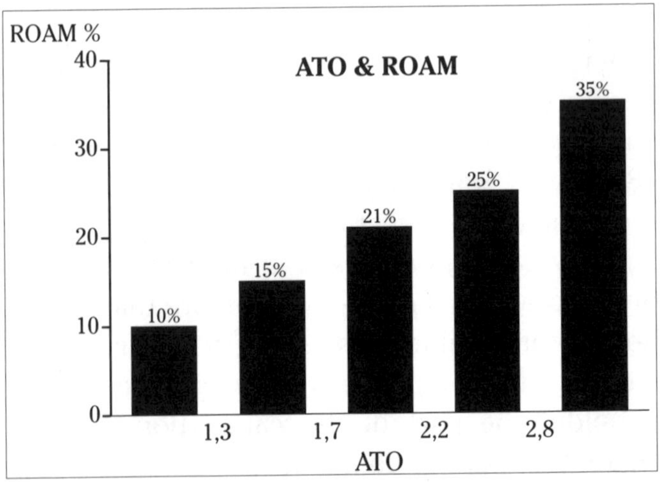

spin your assets when you beat a turn of 2. That's when you generate a good ROAM. Where is MDS on the curve?'

'It's right where this chart shows it would be – at the bottom of the scale. With an ATO of less than 1, they have a ROAM of 8%. It's clear, *ATO makes, or breaks, your ROAM!*'

'Yes, it doesn't matter what business you have. You can't beat the odds, Simon. So, let us pose a question about the $3 billion of "intangible assets". What do they say about it in the notes?'

'They bought a company called ComputeX. Based on assets, it had a value of about $100 million.'

'Was it making any profit?'

'No. It lost money last year.'

'What did they pay for it?'

'More than $2 billion!'

'Wow ... now *that* is bewildering.'

'That's not all. They paid more than $700 million for other companies with assets valued at about $20 million. It all adds up to the "goodwill"of $3 billion! What is going on? Do they know something about these companies that we don't? I'm starting to think they may be chumps.'

'Simon, we might be the chumps, and naïve to boot, because the whole world gives these guys, and others like them, many awards for this and that. Mr Cole's face is forever on the cover of magazines and in newspapers. Maybe we hold the wrong end of the stick and they do know things that we don't, but that's what you'll test.'

'You make me nervous.'

'Don't be. If you're well prepared, they'll treat you with courtesy. Even if you touch a raw nerve, and you most likely will, they'll be polite but pretend you don't understand how the world works, which is probably true. It's a mystery to me.'

'I don't believe they'll even see me let alone give me a job after this.'

'You could be right, but are you still keen enough to try?'

'Yes.'

'Great! Before you go ahead with the letter, as these intangible numbers are very big indeed, let us include them in your calculations. If we add in all the goodwill, what does that do?'

Simon quickly does the sum and says, 'ATO slows right down to 0,3 and the ROAM to less than 4%.'

'Aha! That's your DAZZGOTO!'

'How come?'

'*Their low* ATO *will upset the apple cart.* Today, for every $1 of assets, they generate 30 cents in sales. They paid way too much for these companies and now need more than three years to turn the assets just once. They're heading for big trouble.'

'Are you serious?'

'Very … and using our golf swing analogy, they've swung themselves off their feet. They play an unbalanced, high-risk, low-return game. Like my golf, they now visit parts of the course they've never seen before.'

Simon smiles, then asks, 'But how do we handle the issue of "intangible" and "tangible" assets?'

'Let's think about that … what's the difference between them?'

'The tangible ones are physical. You can see and touch them. Intangible ones you can't.'

'What are these intangible ones?'

'The "goodwill" they paid for companies they bought. They don't invent, design or make anything, so they don't have patents. There is also "brand equity". They talk about it but don't value it on the balance sheet.'

'What is the *one* thing all these types of asset have in common?'

'They have to create sales.'

'Exactly!'

'Shall I include the goodwill in my calculations, then?'

'Why not? They claim to be a "brainy" company, so you have to know if the brains get out of bed in the morning or lounge around between the ears all day.'

'What's the next step, then?'

'Without a context, numbers don't mean much. Take these and turn them into simple run and bar charts. With those in front of you, writing your letter will be easy.'

'They'll be ready before the day's out.'

'Wonderful! It's Wednesday today. If you can get it done and delivered on Friday, Cole will have it in hand on Monday when he returns from his golf tournament. It should give him a wake-up call.'

Later that day they get together again.

'OK, let's see what you've done,' says his Dad eagerly. He looks at the charts silently for a few moments then says, 'You'll knock his socks off with these.'

Simon looks proudly at his handiwork and asks, 'Do you really think so?'

'He may even start smoking them. This is a "new economy" company. They pride themselves on state-of-the-art systems that crunch out numbers at the speed of light. However, I bet they never get to see data presented like this. Most of their numbers are still "data", not information.'

'What do you mean?'

'People generate data to understand what's

going on. You understand only when the data is transformed into information. To achieve that, you need a context. *Plot data points* and you create one. The golden rule is *judge a trend* – not the isolated number. Trends tell a story and raise questions that lead to insight. Let's list some and then you can write your letter.' They talk a while more, then Simon works a couple of hours before he shares his handiwork again.

'Brilliant,' says his Dad, 'With few words, four simple charts, and one, big, clear idea, you will alert Cole to the effects of his actions. That's a damn sight more than his financial guys, board of directors, or market analysts have ever done. Instead of a sycophantic fan club, this is an owner of the business sending a clarion call to arms. It is a most powerful message carried by a most unlikely messenger.'

Sometimes Simon has no clue what his Dad is talking about. It sounds as if big corporations do strange things at times, so he humours him by listening quietly and then asks, 'Shall I take it round to their offices, then?'

'Definitely. Get it there before close of business tomorrow. Address it "Personal" and "By Hand". He should have it on his desk Monday morning. That's if some bureaucrat doesn't hijack it first. Then we wait to see what happens.'

'Just wait?'

'No, get yourself down to the golf club and cast your net out. You need options. With this message, don't bank on these guys making you an offer.'

'Do you believe that's how they'll react?'

'Who knows? Messengers who bring bad news are often shot by the people who *should* be shot. They can't shoot you, but they won't fall over themselves to thank you. That's definite, so just remember the goal. Are we learning?'

'Yes, and we did say that even if I went to HR, I'd be wasting my time. I'll get it there today.'

'Great, I'm proud of you,' his Dad says. 'But one last thing …'

'What?'

'The "swing thought" … what must your one "swing thought" be?'

Simon laughs and says, 'Balance, Dad … balance is the key!'

'That's my boy! You'll be a scratch man before the year's out.'

4. *'They all laughed!'*

Simon says disconsolately one morning, 'It's been two weeks since I delivered the letter … still no reply. It looks as if all my friends are right.'

'What do you mean? A lot has happened. You've got your first job and all on your own. That's fantastic. Now you have to perform and learn as much as you can there. But what's this about your friends?'

'They all laughed. They say there's no way the chairman of MDS will see me.'

'We know it is a long shot to play, but I believe he'll respond. People say he's a great guy, so give him the benefit of the doubt. Mind you, there's a good chance he ignores your letter and hopes you go away. Maybe somebody waylaid it after all. Phone them and ask if it reached his office. Remember, you are a shareholder. They owe you the courtesy of a reply at least.'

Simon phones them and comes back to say, 'His secretary says it never arrived, so I'll e-mail another.'

'I bet someone binned it. Didn't I warn you?

Besides, who are you, a student, to question the chairman and then ask for a job? Who do you think you are?'

They laugh, but a day after e-mailing another copy, Simon yells from the PC, 'Hey, Dad! Guess what? There's a message from Cole's office to say he'll see me a week today. Help! What do I do now?'

'Panic gently, Simon … panic gently!'

'Seriously, how do I handle this?'

'Well, what's the one thing we agree to keep uppermost in mind?'

'That I'm a shareholder.'

'And a rookie at that. It means you can ask the dumb questions. Secondly, what is the DAZZGOTO in your letter?'

'The low ATO they caused could bring the value of the company crashing down sooner or later.'

'Yes, and it has nothing to do with market conditions or the economy.'

'So that's my approach then?'

'Definitely. You've taken dead aim and pitched the ball up against the stick for a dead cert birdie. Now it's their turn to play. Your simple ROAM analysis of the business raises tough questions. One of them is a nutcracker. You are a student and a shareholder who expects some answers. They are highly respected businessmen. See if they can explain themselves. You don't have to do a thing except run through your questions before you go.'

'OK,' says Simon, 'but you make it sound so easy.'

'Your blood pressure will rise and your pulse will race but you aren't going in as a "know-all". You want to learn from them because they have achieved a lot. Just be yourself. To prepare, explain and test your thoughts with some of your friends. Until you say what you think, you don't know what you think.'

'That's exactly what I'll do,' Simon says, and he does. His friends still cannot understand how he has gained entry to the chairman's office but maybe that's because, like many others, they do not grasp how significant his message is.

A week later, he arrives home after the meeting with MDS. His Dad sees the disappointed expression on his face and asks, 'So, what happened?'

'They were really polite and pleasant to me, but I expected more, I guess,' says Simon with a sigh.

'Run me through it.'

'Well, I arrive at the chairman's office. He is a very nice guy indeed. I really like him. "Hi, Simon," he says, "call me James. We're all on first names in this company." Then we discuss sport, golf, where I went to school, what I study now. It is all very friendly and relaxed. Then he asks what I wish to discuss, so I pull out my charts. As soon as I hit the Asset Turnover issue and buying all these companies, he says, "Simon, we don't buy assets, we buy people."

'So I say, "Fine, but what about the $3 billion goodwill? That's a lot of potatoes to invest. Shouldn't we be getting a return on it?" Then he says, "Wait a second."

'He hauls off and wheels in another very nice guy, Max Ford, who is the head of Finance. He is also a fine golfer, and very genial, so we talk a little about this and that and have a few laughs.

'Before long we get back to my question, and Max says, "Simon, you must understand, we are in the people business. We have intellectual capital, so ROAM does not apply to us. That's an old economy measure for bricks-and-mortar companies that make things."

'I do not know what he talks about, so I stick to my guns and repeat the question: 'But if we pay $3 billion for these companies, or people as you put it, shouldn't we be making a return on that investment of $3 billion?'

'Max then says, "Talk to one of my staff. He has the time to explain how the business works. He will answer all your questions. Come back when you have your degree, and then we can talk about a job."

'They wheel me out, and the next thing I am in front of a young chartered accountant called Angus Scott who has the cool title Vice President Group Finance.

'He seems more open with me because when I show him my charts he says, "Simon, you are right in some ways. We had to allay the concerns of a merchant bank only two weeks ago. They were worried about whether we could meet our profit forecast. We do have a few problems in some of our international operations, but we are fixing them as we speak."

'I say that is not what I am trying to tell them, but soon he politely shows me the door. He tells me to keep in touch, but in the end, they say nothing. It's all a big disappointment to me.'

'Hey, I know we aimed high. The main purpose is to learn and build your confidence. You are hurt because they seemed to take your questions lightly and did not offer you a position – one you don't need now anyway. Right?'

'Right,' agrees Simon.

'Think about your meeting. Put yourself in their shoes – management ones this time. Did they answer you? I mean, *really* answer you, a *shareholder*?'

'No.'

'Why not?'

'Maybe they can't.'

'You're right. Your questions are very tough, and if they can't respond to them, how do they handle this irritating problem – "Simon the trouble-making shareholder"?'

'I'm not sure.'

'How about they hope you go away and leave them to think about the issues you raise? Then, if they don't know how to handle them, how about they downplay your whole argument as irrelevant? Isn't that exactly what they've done?'

'Yes, I guess it is.'

'Simon, you have just seen the leader of the MDS global empire and some of his courtiers. What children's tale does this remind you of? Do you remember some of the bedtime stories we used to read together? The one about the little boy sitting on his father's shoulders watching the royal procession go by ...?'

'The emperor and his new clothes!'

'That's the one. So what's one thing we have learned so far?'

'Like the clothes, the "goodwill" isn't there!'

'Or, he played a "fresh air" shot, missed the ball and hoped no one saw it!' They laugh, and then his father presses him more. 'What else?' he asks.

'These guys do not use the ROAM measure.'

'True, but what else have you learned and discovered?'

'Well, I know more about ROAM and MDS than I did before.'

'OK, but what has that done for you? How did you feel walking in there?'

'Very nervous.'

'And then?'

'Still unsure of myself because this is all new to me, and I couldn't seem to get them to understand.'

'Look, this was not easy for you,' his Dad says, 'but then?'

'I suddenly knew I had touched that raw nerve you talked of, and felt more confident.'

'Now we're getting warmer ... how come?'

'Cole made a quiet comment to Max as I was leaving to see Angus. He said: "I wonder what a major institutional investor would say about this." And you know what ... despite their fame and success, that's when I knew they aren't as strong as they pretend to be, and I am not as weak as they want me to believe!'

'That's it! If we get nothing else out of the project, it has been worthwhile just for one thing – building up your confidence. You've already grown.'

'You mean you don't care about the job? Thanks a lot ... I thought this was a team effort to get me into MDS!'

They laugh, and his Dad says, 'That hasn't worked so far, I admit. However, you still have to respond to them. So let's prepare for that. We'll start this weekend.'

'Great,' says Simon, and he goes off humming, 'Ol' King Cole was a merry ol' soul and a merry ol' soul was he … he called for his pipe in the middle of the night and a ROAM of 33!'

5. *'Low ATO means stormy weather!'*

The next Saturday they get to work again, and his Dad says, 'Simon, you have done Cole and his men a very big favour even if they don't know it yet.'

'What's that?'

'You have confronted them with a huge problem of their own making. As you know, it is never easy to face up to problems we create for ourselves. It's hard for all of us, but especially them.'

'What do you mean?'

'Business is a deadly serious game, and people at the top take themselves very, very seriously indeed. Guys with power don't like to learn because they think they don't have to. Now you come along and show them that the low ATO they caused puts them in deep, deep trouble. Their egos could get in the way of them doing anything about it.'

'Does this happen often?'

'Yes. Egos are the root cause of most disasters, and their low ATO is a beauty. However, all of us, including them, can learn a lot from it and turn it to advantage. Here, let me show you what happens to ROS and ROAM when ATO is low,' he says, and draws a model on a pad as he speaks.

'Say a top management team of a typical manufacturing company persuades its board to back a

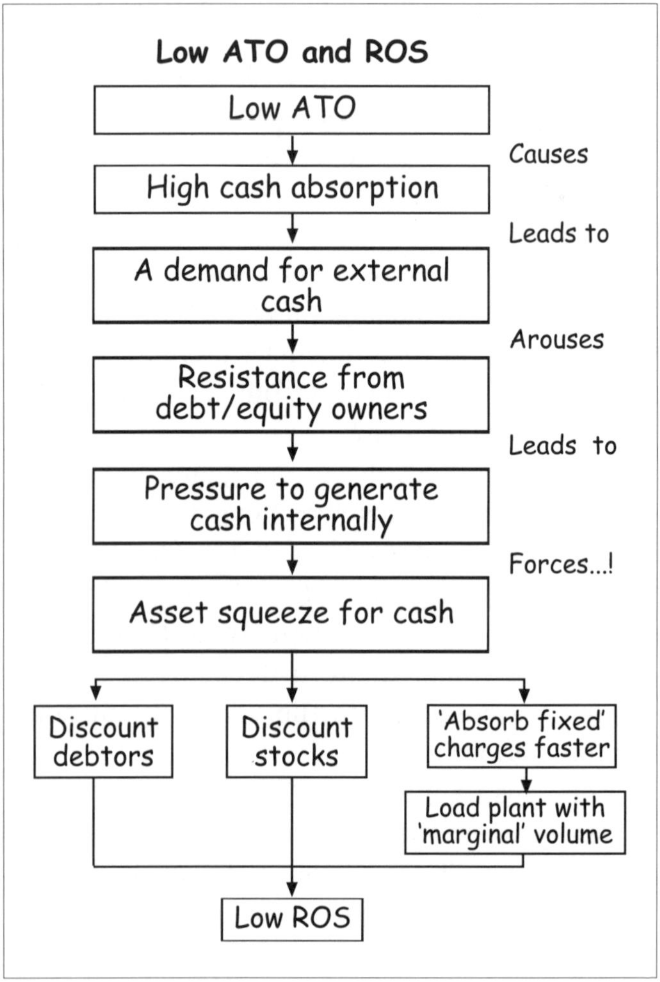

big project. To justify the millions they spend on new plant and equipment, managers eagerly find ways to keep it busy. They always assume volumes are the key to returns, so inventory piles up, as do accounts receivable. The result is a low ATO.'

'Why does that happen?'

'Inventory rises because production people get busy making enough product to meet the sales forecasts that top managers promised but are not achieving. Then, because so many products lie in the warehouse ready for sale, the marketing manager gives extended credit terms to customers to get them to buy. They take longer and longer to pay. All this means more assets and the need for more cash. Next, they take a begging bowl to owners and lenders, who tell them to get off their "assets" and squeeze cash out of them instead.'

'How do they go about that?'

'They reduce prices to get customers to buy and induce them to pay with bigger settlement discounts. So what do you think competitors do?'

'I guess they react in the same way to protect themselves.'

'Exactly, so competition degenerates into a volume-grubbing contest. They pump even more volume through the plant to reduce "overhead" costs per unit. Then they sell products at a "marginal" profit to recover costs.'

'That's "accounting-speak" for no profit, isn't it?' Simon says.

'Yes, and the trouble is, everyone else starts playing the same game. A once-off pricing strategy becomes the normal way of doing business. EBIT vanishes like the early morning mist and down go ROS and ROAM. They "write down" inventory value to zero and lay off people by the thousand, to the delight of financial analysts who think that's what productivity is all about. Morale drops, and the experience is a very bitter one for one company after another. There's a lot of blood on the ground, and it was top management actions that caused all the bleeding in the first place – not the people who do the work!'

'But MDS doesn't own factory buildings, plant and machinery. It doesn't make anything. It's a "new economy" company,' says Simon.

'There are no "old economy" or "new economy" companies – there are only "good" or "bad" ones, and these guys used "financial engineering" instead to build a huge asset base. To make it worse, it's a "fixed", inflexible one – just like land, buildings, plant and equipment. They paid massive premiums for the companies they bought, and now show it as "goodwill". As you rightly pointed out, you expect them to make a reasonable return on it. To make matters worse, their ATO for inventory and receivables has almost halved. So even their operating productivity is bad today.'

'OK, so are you saying they fit this model you drew there ... that their ROS will start falling too?'

'It's as inevitable as the sunrise and sunset. With a low ATO, you can predict what's coming. It's like a barometer.'

'I said I expect them to generate a return on the "goodwill" but this sudden plunge to a low ATO means stormy weather is on the way. They can't escape it. How will that affect me?'

'Let's test that now, and then you'll be able to write to them again.'

6. *'Hey, I'm last in the queue!'*

As they get down to it again, his Dad says, 'Simon, you asked King Cole for a return on the "goodwill" they paid. They seem to have skirted round this key issue: *Cash is at the core of all business activity.*'

'What does that mean?'

'It isn't enough to generate a profit. All a "profit" tells you is that your selling prices recover the *normal* costs of doing business. There are two flaws to testing the health of a firm this way:

1. Profit is the result of crunching numbers with methods that ignore cash.
2. Most managers think that *your cash*, owner's equity, is *free* money[2]. It isn't, but this misguided belief governs their behaviour.'

'How do we address cash, then?'

'At the end of each month we have to pay a lot of people. Before we identify who they are, and you are one of them, let's tackle the second flaw first.'

'OK, so are you saying that I should be charging Ol' King Cole for my money?'

'Yes, and the cost is a lot more than managers think it is.'

'How do I calculate it?'

'Well, you can't commit the *same* cash to two or more businesses at the same time. Imagine you face a number of doors. Each of them opens onto a different investment opportunity for you. One opens onto MDS. If you choose it, you abandon any other opportunity. By opening and entering one door, you *slam shut all other doors* for your cash.'

'I never thought of it like that.'

'In a real, practical sense, you make a *sacrifice*. You sacrifice the opportunity for dividends and share value growth that lie behind the other doors now slammed shut. That's the 'cost-of-equity'. You have to calculate what it is and charge them for it.'

'How do I do that?'

'The best way is to look at other companies, see how they perform, and then decide. Don't over-analyse it. Look for a reasonable middle way that everyone can accept. Work out what percent return you want, and see how Cole and his team perform against your expectation.'

'OK, but is there a quick and easy way for me to do that?' Simon asks.

'Sure, look at this financial magazine. It lists all the top companies on the Stock Exchange with their results over time. You can pick out the best returns on shareholder equity over five years. OK?'

Simon nods, and his Dad continues, 'Your "cost-of-equity" is part of the "cost-of-capital". The other part comes from the decision to *borrow* money that has to be repaid. The lender demands interest payments until you pay back the loan. This charge rewards the lender for *his* sacrifice. He's in the same boat as you are. Once he lends the money to one borrower, he too slams shut all the other doors he could have entered with his cash. This is the "cost-of-debt". It isn't as expensive as owner's money because you can charge it against tax. That's why companies do borrow money. The two added together make up the total "cost-of-capital".'

'So how do I know if MDS makes enough money and generates enough cash?'

'Usually, at the end of every month, management opens up a cash payout window. *It uses cash it collected from customers and banked* before month-end. It has to pay eager, often aggressive, lobby groups who elbow their way into the "queue-for-cash" lined up outside. It's a case of *first-come-first-served*! Each contender-for-cash shouts to be paid first and shoves his way, by whatever means, as close to the head of the queue as he can get.'

'So who does head up the queue?'

'Usually you invite COGS to the front.'

'Why?'

'Because if you don't pay your suppliers promptly and regularly, it's a quick way to stall the whole business.'

'Remind me what COGS also includes.'

'They are *all the costs* of bringing your product or service to the stage where it is *"ready-for-sale"*. These include materials, packaging, wages and *all the waste, rework and scrap* caused by people and the system. They add up to "Cost-of-Goods Sold" (COGS).'

'OK, so what's next?'

'The Operating Expenses (OPEX) that come from servicing customers competitively. This is where you find "accounting" charges like "depreciation". Take all of these accounting adjustments out. They aren't cash costs. Value everything at the cash cost to the business, and that includes the assets. That's how you overcome the accounting flaws.'

'Will I be able to do that with MDS?'

'Well enough for what we want to do, but we'll get to that. Also within OPEX are the "costs-of-the-future". These are research, development, re-design, training, patent protection and so on. You spend them to grow the company and stay in business.'

'I suppose they cut those when the company hits trouble.'

'Yes, often there isn't enough cash left over to

meet all demands of the business. They can't hold their position, and they disappear from the scene. Next in the queue are your lenders. You pay them their "cost-of-debt". The taxman follows, with his "cost-of-tax".'

'And then there's me, the shareholder ... I'm last in the queue-for-cash ... I should be first ... everyone else is playing out of turn!'

'Dead right. "Owners" are so far back that most managers forget them. There they wait patiently, cap-in-hand, out of sight, out of mind. If there is any cash left, they try to keep you happy with a part-payment. They call them dividends. Often, they reduce the payout or give nothing at all because there isn't enough cash to meet the other pressing demands they have. Sometimes they even borrow more cash to pay you something. In the end, this undermines and destroys your confidence and commitment to them.'

'But I've never been paid by MDS,' Simon says.

'True, but instead, the value of your stock has climbed high because these guys have grown profits and sales so much. That's what excites market analysts and investors. You enjoyed the rise in value, but can MDS sustain it? It could vanish like a "will o' the wisp".'

'You mean because of the issues we raise?'

'Yes,' his Dad says. 'We can see that to grow

fast, and keep growing, they buy mediocre companies and pay far too much for them.'

He pauses, and then says, 'Hey, Simon, talking about analysts, there's something we should do before you reply. Get hold of that friend of yours who joined that famous merchant bank. Their analysts must have done a review for the start of the year. Ask him for it.'

'OK, I'll see if I can collect one tomorrow.'

He brought it home the next evening …

The Queue-for-Cash	**$(000s)**
IN: Sales-in-cash-*banked*!	
1. **OUT**: 'Ready-for-sale' COGS	
IN: Gross profit	________
2. **Out**: OPEX & 'Costs-of-the-future'	
IN: EBIT	________
3. **OUT**: 'Cost-of-debt'	
IN: Profit before tax	________
4. **OUT**: 'Cost-of-tax'	
IN: Profit-after-tax	________
5. **OUT**: Owner's 'Cost-of-equity'	
IN: Economic profit or loss	________

Plug in the numbers … do you run out of cash before the owner reaches the payout window?

7. *'Hey, you've done it again!'*

As Simon hands the report over, his Dad asks, 'What does their analyst have to say?'

'He recommends people to buy the stock and ends by saying that MDS creates economic value. What's that?'

'It's what we talked about yesterday – the cost-of-capital (COC). Unless a business returns a profit greater than its COC, it operates at a loss. The profit over the COC is what they call "economic value" or "economic profit".'

'So it's what's left over after paying me and everyone else in the "queue-for-cash", right?'

'Exactly.'

'It doesn't seem as if MDS can make an economic profit, does it?'

'Not from what we've seen. I bet they make a huge economic loss, and the message you have to get through to them is that *ATO drives the creation of economic value.*'

'What about this analyst?'

'Like many of them, he is no better than "Hot Horse Herbie!"'

'Who's he?'

'A Damon Runyon character who lurks around the race tracks with stories about horses that cannot lose unless they drop down dead. This man writes rubbish. Do the calculations, then if they come out as we expect them to, contact him.'

'Isn't the calculation complicated?'

'We'll keep it simple, and you won't be far off what the experts calculate. Use your "queue-for-cash" with the MDS numbers we have. When you get to the payout window, see how far short they are.'

Simon goes off with the latest annual report to work it out. It doesn't take long.

'Here it is,' he says a short while later. 'I used their EBIT, or operating profit number. They paid no interest but received some. I added that to the profit, and after tax it came to a return on shareholder's equity of about 4%.'

'What return do you expect?'

'At least 20%.'

'That sounds fair. What's the "economic loss" then?'

'More than $600 million!'

'Ouch! That's for only one year of trading, too. Do it for the last four years and show the cumulative effect. It'll be horrific next year.'

'Shall I send all my work to this guy?'

'Definitely. Ask him how he reaches his conclusions and for a meeting to discuss them. He is dangerous to the health of the investment community.'

Days go by, and the press reports certain events along the way. MDS wins a 'Growth' award judged by world-famous accountants and management consultants. MDS directors sell some of their stock. The proceeds net them more than a bob or two which some people consider fair given the years of good returns for shareholders up to then.

However, this 'profit-taking' upsets more than a few punters. The share price tumbles a bit afterwards and some 'marquee' IT companies, including Cisco no less, announce profit warnings.

For a while the year before, Cisco was the world's most valuable company. *Fortune* magazine and analysts even wonder if its CEO isn't the greatest manager in history. Today, they are not so sure about that any more.

To allay fears raised because of its links with companies like Cisco, MDS announces it has no problem meeting its own forecasts.

The analyst eventually replies by e-mail, saying he does not know the ROAM model and that he is 'too busy' to spare the time for a discussion.

One Sunday a while later, Simon feels he is

now ready to write and thank Mr Cole for taking the time to see him. It so happens that he spots an article in the paper that day about a company MDS buys in the USA. They pay $140 million for a firm with assets of $20 million. Moreover, it does not make much money. He works out that it will take them more than 30 years to recover the cash at the current level of profit.

'Hey, Dad,' he calls out, 'they're still at it. They're buying another company for a big premium.'

'So what will you do about it?'

'Tell 'em, I guess.'

'Good. It's time to reply. A lot has happened in a few weeks, and you have learned much more since meeting them. You can make them think even harder now.'

Simon writes another well-crafted letter. He is proud of this one too.

19 March 01

Dear Mr Cole

Thank you for seeing me. My talks with you, Max Ford and Angus Scott were interesting. However, it puzzles me that you feel the points I raise do not apply to MDS. The current share price fall has nothing to do with what I am getting at.

I still think the money spent over the

last two years to buy 'people not assets', as you put it, will come back to haunt you. You paid a lot for those companies. Now I see you have done it again.

You bought Premier Integrity Systems (PIS) in the USA and paid $140 million. That's seven times the asset value of the company.

The only plus is that PIS must have a higher ROAM than MDS, but still a very low one. With its profit today of $3,7 million before tax on sales of $150 million, you will never recover the cost-of-capital. You paid far too much.

MDS's ATO has plunged. As it seems to drive company value, I am concerned. I hope things are not as bad as they seem to be.

I learned a bit more after we met. One of you asked when looking at my charts, 'How would major investors react to this analysis?' You asked that question because their response affects the share price and value of the firm.

As a shareholder, I discovered that I can affect the share price in only two ways:

1. My 'cost-of-capital' – the return I expect for investing my cash with you.
2. My belief that you can use my cash to

generate returns higher than my 'cost-of-capital'.

You say neither ROAM, nor beating a 'cost-of-capital' target, apply to MDS because it is a 'new economy' company. That troubles me, but so far, it doesn't trouble market analysts. It seems you can keep them happy with continued sales and profit growth. As to productivity, they seem to get excited and reward companies with a better stock price only when they lay off thousands of people.

However, if asset productivity, especially ATO, drives value then it is only a matter of time before your major investors wake up. When they see the size of the shortfall to recover the cost-of-capital, they will react.

I include this chart to show that you have launched MDS onto a plummeting value-destruction curve.

The picture may be even worse because my cost-of-capital target is only 20%. It may be too low because you have no debt. What return would you expect on your equity?

Only a ROAM of about 20% can recover the cost-of-capital. You used to

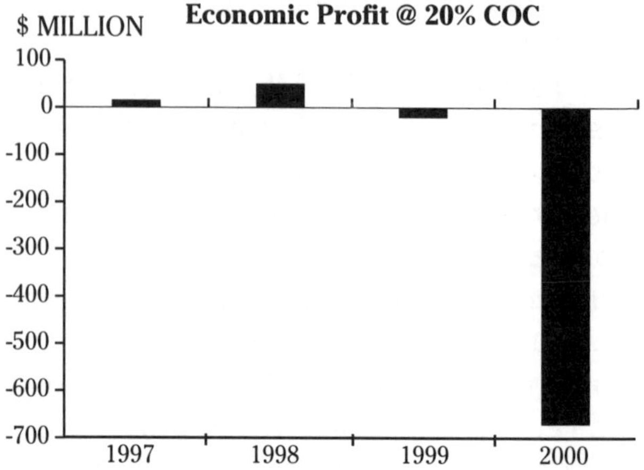

achieve that. Even if you deduct all the goodwill, your ROAM is still only 8%. With today's asset base, you need an EBIT of more than $1 billion. On sales of $2 billion that is a tall order, isn't it? The graph will be even worse next year. The value destruction number is cumulative. When you add this year's shortfall to next year's, it will not be a pretty picture.

Thanks again for taking time to see me. Few people at your level would do that. I hope we meet again, even if it is only on the golf course!

Yours sincerely
Simon Raikes

'Simon, this is another mortar bomb. Are you sure you want to lob it into his office?'

'I can't chicken out now. You've cost me a job there already.'

They both laugh and Simon says, 'The trouble is I still don't know what to do about my MDS shares. Shall I talk to friends I have in the stock broking business and hear what they have to say?'

'It's always valuable to get other views. But in the end, it'll be your call.'

Despite his analysis of MDS, Simon looks unsure. Can his point of view be the correct one? In the face of opinions made by very influential people, is MDS really heading for a brick wall?

8. *'Your relative, competitive ATO decides the contest!'*

Only two days pass before Simon calls out from the PC, 'Hey, guess what? Max Ford wants to see me. He says he'd like to look at my stuff again because he's a "bit rusty" on some of it!'

'There you go. Isn't that amazing?'

'Yes, but how do I handle him? All this stuff is still so new to me.'

'That's why this project is such a great learning opportunity.'

Simon sighs, 'This isn't what I had in mind when we started. It's a bit scary rocking around at the top of MDS!'

'To prepare and reduce your concern, why don't you see the dean of your college Prof. Andrew James? He will enjoy your work and give interesting insight on the issues.'

'I will,' Simon says. A few days later, he arrives at the business college to meet him. He walks into a spacious office surrounded by shelves from floor to ceiling. They overflow with business books and magazines.

The dean beams a warm smile of welcome as he gets up from his desk. 'Good to see you,

Simon,' he says, 'let's sit over there.' He motions to a couch at a low table. It faces open doors and overlooks lush, rolling lawns that slope down to a river meandering lazily alongside the beautiful campus.

'How can I help? You have an exciting project on the go, you tell me.'

'Yes, and I know it will interest you.'

'It sounds mysterious. Fire away.'

Simon briefly recounts the events so far, and then gives the dean his letters and flowchart to look at.

He reads them through silently, chuckles, and then smiles broadly, saying, 'This shows brass. I see why you grabbed their attention.'

'The financial director wants to see me again, but I'm not sure why. He says he's rusty on these measures.'

'Rusty? I guess that's one way of putting it. They've forgotten why they did so successfully in the early days. If Cole sold routers from the boot of his car, he knows exactly what ATO means because the basic rules of business have not changed since the days of the pharaohs.'

He pauses, then says, 'You may ask: "What are some of these basic rules?"'

Simon nods and the dean continues, 'There are a handful, but the only way for a business to be secure is to make money and generate cash.'

'Like a cash-compounding machine,' Simon says, recalling earlier discussions.

'Exactly, and the company's asset base is the engine room. However, a business is a lot more than that because of its people. A good analogy is Planet Earth, which works on ratios and a continuous process of renewal. If you violate that principle, you squander resources on a grand scale – human, physical and cash. The costs can be huge. They always spell disaster.'

'Are you saying that could happen to MDS?'

'Yes, because there is only one way to create value and secure your strategic position in the market place. You have to improve productivity in a *sustainable* way, year on year. What you show through your ROAM analysis is that they now do the opposite. Only managers make resources productive, and *input:output ratios* are the *only valid measures* of their intent, and results. The ROAM model contains some key ones, but ATO is the most important. At MDS today the ratios all seem to be heading south.'

He continues, 'If a business is a cash-compounding machine, then the *CTC Cycle* is its *engine*.'

'What's the CTC Cycle?'

'Of the handful of business rules, the *only* 'Business Success *Imperative*' is the *Cash-to-Cash Cycle*. It is the *compounding velocity*, the speed of the *CTC Cycle* that governs whether a business survives or not. I call it *asset spin.*'

'That's ATO, is it?'

'Yes, it's the engine. You have to get it *spinning smoothly* instead of grinding over slowly.'

'What's the fuel?'

'Customer service – delivering *measurable value*. The truth is that marketing managers and consultants spout a constant stream of drivel about the customer being 'king' or 'queen'. Clearly, customers are important. You wouldn't have a business without them, but in the end, *your relative competitive ATO decides the contest.* Nothing else does. This is the crunch question managers have to ask themselves: *How do we give better service than our competitors but make sure that our ATO is always faster than theirs? Not perfect service, just better service – not a hugely faster ATO, just one that we can sustain. 10% faster will do just fine.*'

'Why does that ensure you win?'

'Look at the research. *Asset spin* drives up ROAM because it drives up ROS!'[3]

'How does it do that?'

'In all companies they reckon people spend 5% or less of their working time adding value. That means for 95% of the time, even more, they add costs[4]. If you can speed up ATO, the *CTC Cycle*, what will it mean?'

Simon thinks for a moment, then says, 'I guess

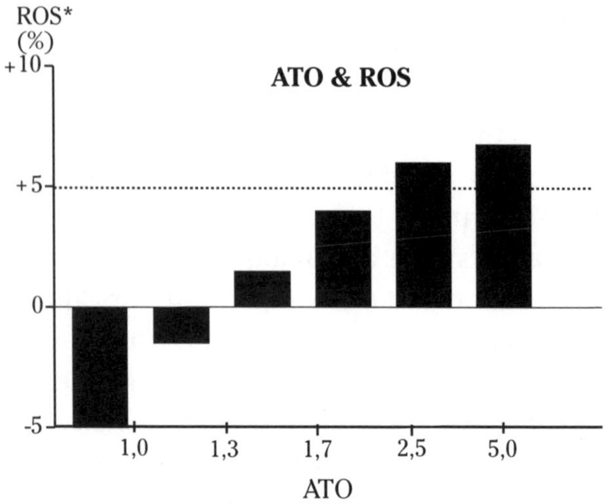

- Returns rise steadily from left to right.
- With low ATO you will most probably record a loss before tax.
- ATO has a powerful, 'hidden' effect.

*This is ROS after an interest charge.

it's like finishing a golf shot in perfect balance. You must have made a good swing. If you can get results faster, it means you do the right things. You eliminate mistakes and remove delays in the system all along the way from start to finish. That lowers costs. Your service and sales improve, and customers pay you quicker because they have no excuses not to.'

'Yes, it's that simple. Research from around the world proves it repeatedly[5] – a higher relative ATO gives you a huge advantage. It also reduces costs and drives up ROS. It raises some very strong defensive barriers.'

'Like what?'

'Firstly, it's *invisible.* Competitors know your selling prices and can make good estimates of your margins. However, they don't know what your ATOs are. They are much harder to find out.'

'Secondly?'

'It's *price insensitive* – you can ship products at a lower price than your competitors because you can achieve the same ROAM with a lower ROS when your ATO is higher than theirs. It's a cash shield when a competitor starts a price war. If your ATO is higher, you can bleed longer. It also means you can *smooth and ease downturns* by generating a respectable ROAM. Finally, it *protects you in a hostile business climate.* It is the single most important message for any company to think about.'

'So that's it. *Your relative, competitive ATO decides the contest,*' Simon says.

'That's the truth of it.'

'They won't ask me, but if they were to ask you, how should they go about solving this problem that they have created for themselves?' Simon asks.

'There are a few steps to take. Shall I cover them?'
'Yes, please.'

The ATO Shield

$$\frac{\text{YOUR ATO}}{\text{COMPETITOR ATO}} = >1.1$$

- It's invisible and not provocative.
- It's price insensitive.
- It's a cash shield if a price war erupts.
- It smoothes and eases downturns.
- It protects you in a hostile climate.

9. *'Spin your assets in five steps!'*

The dean says, 'With a golf swing, one small change can make a huge difference. It's the same for a company. You can change it with *one* measure. Cole has to light an *asset spin* fire under his business – a high-octane, company-wide asset productivity programme.'

'What will that involve?'

'Ignorance about the basics of business exists at all levels. MDS is proud of its people's technical prowess, but 99% of them are probably still on the bottom rung of the *financial* ladder. They spend money on training, but like all companies, top of its agenda should be an indoctrination programme to educate managers to "Roam" around the business.'

'How do you do it?'

'Refocus managers from "profit centres" to "asset bases". Ask ruthlessly and relentlessly, "*Who owns the assets?*" When you've pinned someone down, make that person responsible for their *value* and the *yield*. Managers make a return on assets – owners make a return on investment.'

'OK, so you want them to think like they "own" the assets,' Simon says, 'but how do you decide what the value is? They seem to have a problem with that.'

'You can do it in at least six ways. The first is *cash cost*. As a shareholder, that's how you want them valued. You expect them to make a return on the cash value of assets.'

'They show EBIT before amortisation and depreciation but not assets.'

'That brings us to the second way – "depreciated" or "amortised" cost. You reduce the value over the asset's useful life. That may make accounting sense with plant and machinery. Not so easy when it comes to "brains", is it?'

'Please don't go down that path! It makes no sense to me.'

The dean laughs, and says, 'Agreed, and we don't need to take that route to find what MDS has to do. Other ways are "replacement" and "market" values.'

'How does the market work?'

'Three ways. First is "going concern" – you estimate a company's future growth in sales and profits, and decide what that makes it worth today. Next, there is "break-up" value. That might happen with a forced sale when a company is in trouble. Lastly, there is "takeover" value. That's what someone will pay to get control.'

'I wonder which method MDS used. It seems as if they'll pay anything to get what they want. What should they do now?'

'Start the programme *today*. Use existing valuation methods with the full knowledge of their disadvantages. More advanced, realistic economic values can come later when people understand more.'

'We already know, without changing anything, that they need a ROAM on total assets of about 20%, right?'

'Correct, but of course there is another radical way to value assets and that's to lease them – charge them to COGS and OPEX. It could be the best option of all.'

'Why?'

'It gives you the true market cost and highlights the potential for redesigning the business.'

'How?'

'This is the second step. The "business model", the way you design and position a business, governs its productivity. *A brilliant business design operated in a mediocre way will knock the socks off a mediocre business design operated brilliantly!*[6] As you well know, with golf, *most mistakes are made before you swing.* Unless your grip, stance, ball position and aim are all correct, you won't play a good shot. It's the same with a business. I have an example from another industry. It's very different from MDS, but everyone can learn from it. It is the tale of two chicken firms – a winner and loser.'

'What was the difference between them?'

'Top management – only top management!'

'In what way?'

'The two management teams looked at the world differently. The losers believed they could control costs by owning almost everything in the value chain of activities. The winners applied the principle of force to gain a powerful lever in their market. They asked themselves an intelligent, incisive question: "*What assets should we own and how do we control the rest?*"'

'What assets are there?'

'In the poultry business, to get a quality bird onto your plate at low cost, you start the whole chain of activity by breeding the best genetic stock. You build up flocks of these birds to lay eggs and produce chicks that you feed and grow for 40 days. You slaughter them and then ship them to cold storage, or direct to supermarkets or fast-food companies. What you have is an industry with lots of assets in land, farms, feed mills, slaughter houses, transport fleets and warehousing.'

'What did the winners do?'

'They pursued their self-interests *without passing the burden*. They did it through *negotiation, co-operation* and *collaboration* along the entire value-cost chain – from suppliers through to customers. First, they have a license agreement and partnership with a world-class poultry-breeding company. This small, strategic investment ensures them high-quality birds. Their major investment is in abattoirs. Almost all other activities they do through supply agreements. They sell chicks to farmers, and feed that they buy from millers. Forty days later they buy back full-grown chickens, slaughter them and ship them. They have a brilliant design and operate it brilliantly.'

'What did the losers do?'

'Almost everything.'

'What was their relative, competitive ATO?'

Prof. James laughed, 'You're learning fast. It was 0,33!'

'Let me guess what they were. The winners had an *asset spin* of 3 and the losers an ATO of 1!'

'Spot on, Simon. Now guess what the ROAMs were.'

'I don't need to,' Simon says. 'Using this research chart, the winners had one of 30% and the losers less than 10%.'

'Right again. In fact, the losers used to top the leader board with a high 25% ROS, and low ATO. The trouble is it is damned hard to sustain a high ROS in the face of hostile competition. They went on to lose hundreds of millions. Only recently have they focussed on an asset spin strategy, and it's starting to work for them.'

'Fascinating. So how do you define this step?'

'*Concentrate* and *focus* with a company *design* that gives you a *competitive* and *responsive* asset mix. One that generates *asset spin*.'

'MDS used to have that, but not today. What you seem to be saying is that if MDS's new business model generates this low ATO, then it can't be any good, can it?'

'What do you think?'

'It looks disastrous! So what's the next step?'

'*Measure the Business Success Imperative – the CTC Cycle*.'

'What goes into that?'

'Look at this model:

'You find these ten assets in most companies. MDS may not have them all, but they need to ask this question: *How long does it take from the time the cash comes in, to the end of the run?*'

'What did you work out the *CTC Cycle* to be for MDS?'

'Just using tangible assets their ATO is 0,7.'

'There are 365 days in the year, so it takes them 256 days to complete one turn of the Assets Managed Wheel. They used to be much faster than that.'

'So what should they do?'

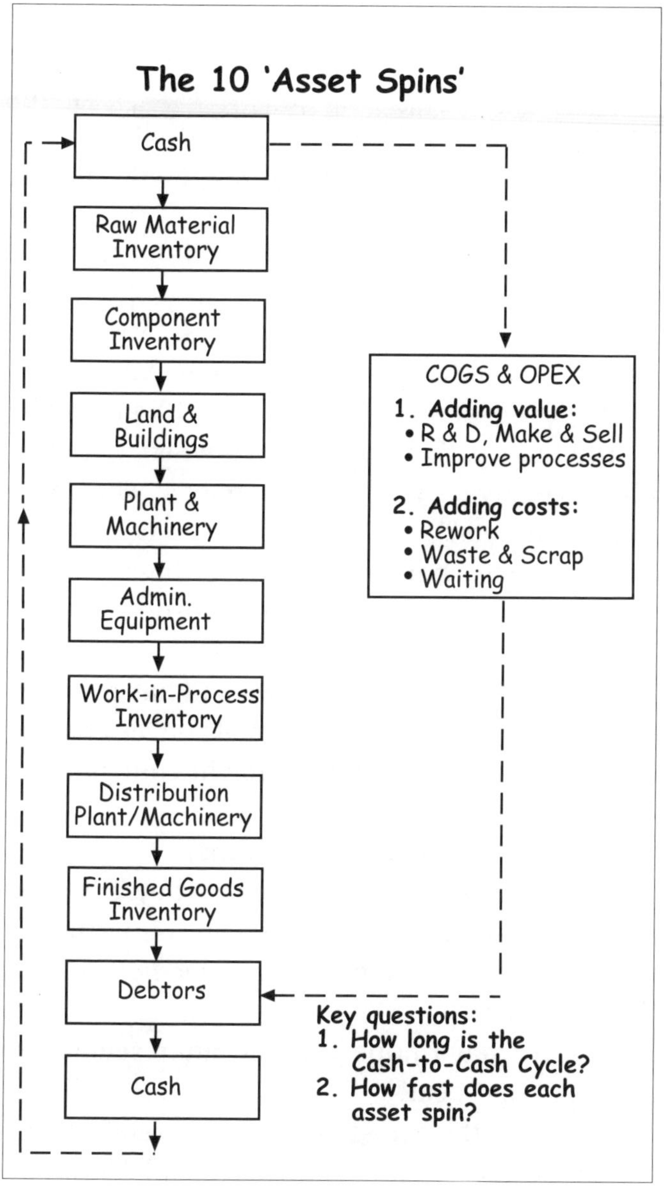
The 10 'Asset Spins'
Cash
Raw Material Inventory
Component Inventory
Land & Buildings
Plant & Machinery
Admin. Equipment
Work-in-Process Inventory
Distribution Plant/Machinery
Finished Goods Inventory
Debtors
Cash
COGS & OPEX
1. Adding value:
• R & D, Make & Sell
• Improve processes
2. Adding costs:
• Rework
• Waste & Scrap
• Waiting
Key questions:
1. How long is the Cash-to-Cash Cycle?
2. How fast does each asset spin?

'Identify each class of asset and ask: *How many $s of sales do we get for this asset*? Pinpoint the significant ones that will strengthen competitive position. Then *measure, graph* and d*ramatise* the data.'

'You mean like I did with Cole without realising what I was doing?'

They laugh, and Prof. James says, 'Absolutely, and if you can do it, so can his financial people.'

'Why have you got COGS and OPEX in there?'

'You tell me. You touched on it when we talked about relative ATO. What happens when you *spin* the assets?'

'Of course, because you do things faster, smoother, with no delays, costs drop and ROS rises.'

'That's what research shows and has done for years. Like golf, the fundamentals never change. Equipment and technology might, but not the fundamentals.'

'OK, so what follows the graphs?'

'Tell them what will happen if they continue down the path they have taken. Show future trends so that they can plan *remedial* or *reinforcing* action.'

'That's what I hope they do after seeing my graphs. What next?'

'Deal with the "most important assets" of all!'

'Let me guess,' Simon laughs. 'People! What do

you do about them? MDS seems to think incentives take care of that.'

'Yes, *reward them for performance*, because you get what you measure and reward. The trouble is that Cole, like many business leaders, seems to believe in stock options. They don't work. People dance to the wrong tune.'

He goes to the flip chart and explains as he writes. 'We'll use just one share to make the point. At the beginning of Year 1 it is worth $10, so opening capital invested is also $10. Let's say management levers a ROAM on assets that generates a 10% ROI for the owners – a Profit After Tax (PAT) of $1. It also gives us "Earnings per Share" (EPS) of $1. That is simple enough, but now they start to play the "EPS" game with the Hot Horse Herbies, as you call the analysts. Managers who understand the rules of this game talk up the value of the share by promising huge growth in sales and earnings. Gullible investors, who believe the hype, are sucked in, and this ratchets up the price to $40 (40 x $1 of EPS). This is called the Price/Earnings Ratio (P-E Ratio). Let's use 40 because that's the kind of multiple people put on shares in companies like MDS. OK so far?'

Simon nods, and the Professor continues. 'Now that people will pay $40 a share, management, encouraged by the Herbies, merchant

Playing the EPS Game!

	Shares #	Capital $	ROI 10% $	EPS $	Share Price (40 x EPS) $	New Shares \#	New Capital $	EPS/ Share Growth
Year 1	1	10	1	1	40	1	40	-
Year 2	2	50 ($40+10)	5	2,50 ($5÷2)	100	1	100	150%
Year 3	3	150 (50+100)	15	5,00 ($15÷3)	200	1	200	100%

bankers and corporate lawyers, who all stand to make money out of them, decide to raise more cash for acquisitions. They do it by issuing and selling another share.

'At the start of Year 2, we now have two shares and capital of $50. The same ROI of 10% generates $5, which gives us EPS of $2,50. Multiply that by 40, the P-E Ratio, and we now have a share price of $100 – a growth in EPS and share price of 150%!'

He continues, 'In Year 3, we start with three shares and capital of $150. ROI stays the same, so that means a profit of $15 and EPS of $5. Multiply that by 40, and what is the share price now?'

'$200!' Simon exclaims.

'Yes, and another 100% growth in EPS and the share price.'

'And what you show up there,' Simon says, 'is that they achieve that huge growth in value with a constant ROI of 10%.'

'That's important, but there's something even more significant. Managers and boards of directors watch EPS, the share price and growth rate rise, but ignore underlying productivity. You see, as long as the ROAM that managers get is high enough to generate ROI that beats the reciprocal of the P-E Ratio, 2,5% (1/40 x 100), the EPS will rise. So, what many companies who chase EPS do is use their own shares to buy indifferent businesses, or they issue shares to raise cash that they invest in low-return projects. You see, as long as they have an ROI that equals, or beats, the 2,5% in our example, they stay in the game. Coincidentally, that level of return seems to fit with MDS's acquisition strategy!'

Professor James hands Simon the pen and says, 'Here, you do the numbers on the chart and see what I mean.'

Simon takes the pen and starts writing. 'In Year 1 we start with one share of $10 and ROI of 2,5%. That gives me 25c profit and 25c EPS.'

'Correct,' says Professor James. 'Now assume the same P-E Ratio of 40. What's the share price?'

'Ten bucks!'

'OK, carry on all the way through like I did,' says James.

Simon does, and it shows that the growth rate in share price and EPS rate stay constant at zero with an ROI of only 2,5%.

Simon's Workings

	Shares #	Capital $	ROI 2,5% $	EPS $	Share Price (40 x EPS) $	New Shares #	New Capital $	EPS/ Share Growth
Year 1	1	10	0,25	0,25	10	1	10	0%
Year 2	2	20	0,50	0,25	10	1	10	0%
		(10+10)		(50÷2)				
Year 3	3	30	0,75	0,25	10	1	10	0%
		(20+10)		(0,75÷3)				

'So what does this mean exactly?' Simon asks.

'Simon, it means that the company ends up with a portfolio of "dogs with fleas". Most companies they buy have low ROAM but just high enough to enhance the EPS. Down comes the overall ROAM and with it, when everyone wakes up to what's going on, shareholder value. They systematically destroy the value-of-the-firm but are encouraged to do it by analysts and merchant bankers!'

'So they punt the share price instead of focussing on productivity. King Cole should be getting his people to focus on asset spin and ROAM, and link incentives to them. Is that all there is to it? Set targets and put them on an incentive scheme?'

'No. Incentives serve a purpose but are little different from using a carrot and stick to get movement. Link the incentives to *personal growth* too.'

'How do you do that?'

'Start management development with a number. After *pinpointing productivity improvement opportunities* along the value-cost chain, turn them into projects that apply learning *just-in-time*, and *on-the-job*. That way you get people to do the work together, and develop relationships and management skills in real situations. You can reward them in many ways for the tangible results they get. Most education and development programmes are no more than a "rain dance". They spend a lot of cash and energy hoping for performance improvement, but the rain never comes.'

'So you're saying *asset spin* and ROAM are all about management development and relationships. Growing people is the "horse", and the "cart" is a ROAM improvement number.'

'Exactly. The prime purpose of the programme is to develop managers and grow people. It's like practising your golf. The improvement in your golf scores tells you how much, and how well, you have practised and learned the right things. To use the golf analogy, you now play the game of business with a simple, balanced swing – people *and* numbers. To summarise, the steps are:

- Refocus managers from "*profit centres*" to "*asset bases*".
- Design a business model with a *competitive* and *responsive asset mix*.

- Measure the *CTC Cycle*.
- Identify *asset spin* performance improvement projects to grow people.
- Gear incentives to *asset spin* and ROAM.

'There you have it. Simple, isn't it?'

Simon sighs and says, 'Phew ... *asset spin* in five steps! Simple maybe, but not so easy to do.'

'No, it isn't, but if they were to take them, they would raise some impregnable competitive strategic productivity barriers. Your projects turn strategy into action. They enable people to learn and apply the fundamentals of business day-to-day. By not paying attention to the fundamentals, companies do more harm to themselves than all their competitors combined. That brings us to the final model I want to show you.'

'Great!'

10. *'Productivity drives positioning!'*

Simon says, 'Take me through this one slowly.' 'Right, the first three measures make you the "lowest cost producer" in your chosen market. *That is always the first goal to achieve. Always!*

1. **Relative Capital Cost per Unit (CCPU)** – take the chicken example ... because the losers had a relative ATO of 0,33, it means they invested *three times* more cash than their competition to produce 1kg of chicken. What has MDS done to its *capital cost per project*?'

'I hate to think!'

'They've put themselves deep in the woods, I can tell you! They can quickly improve their inventory and accounts receivable, though. That's the next barrier:

2. **Relative Marketing ATO** – is MDS's *marketing asset spin* at least 10% higher than its closest competitor? *Spin* the assets and lower your ...
3. **Relative "ready-for-sale" COGS** – are MDS's "ready-for-sale" installation costs lower than any of its competitors?

'The next barrier can only be created if the first three are in place. If you go back to the "queue-for-cash", we have reached the first profit level – gross profit. You want a margin that is big enough to tuck away "costs-of-the-future" like product R&D, training and support systems that enhance customer service, and so on.

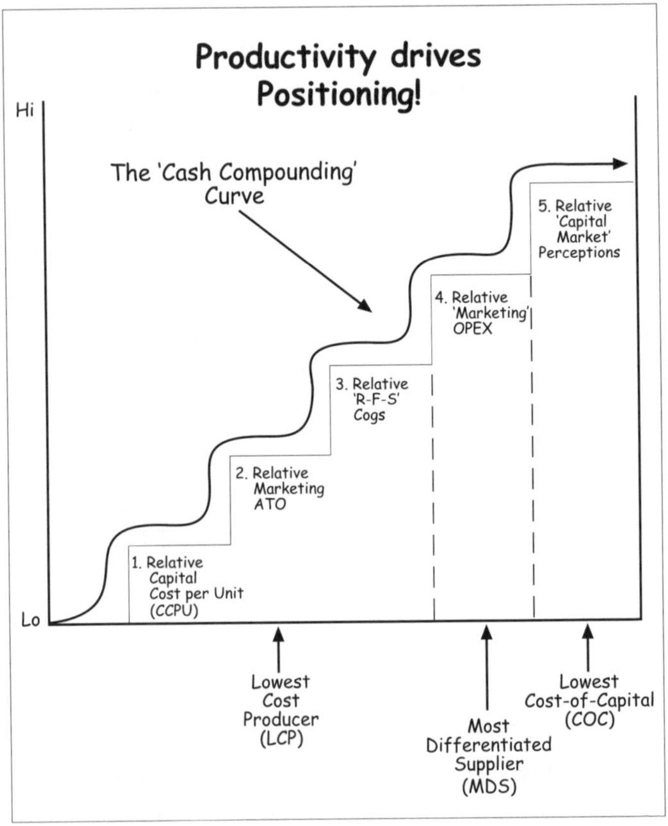

These activities ensure you keep delivering value, grow, and hold your market dominance. It is the fourth barrier …

4. **Relative Marketing OPEX** – Compared to the competition, do we have the cash available to ensure that we stay ahead with our people, technology, products and services? Are we seen as the "most differentiated supplier" – better than any of our direct competitors?

'Lastly, there is...

5. **Relative Capital Market Perceptions** – Are we seen as a "low-risk/high-return" company?'

The dean continues, 'The first four barriers safely "Con-Dom" the business – you *concentrate* resources to *dominate* your market. Superb economic results come from monopolies. That's the aim – to monopolise your chosen market. You don't have to be the biggest overall. *Just be the biggest where you want to be*. Achieve that and investors won't penalise you with a high "cost-of-equity" charge. The "cost-of-capital" is lower. You generate economic profit and make the company ever more valuable – *for everyone* – not just owners.'

'So what you are saying is *productivity drives positioning*. Being good at what you do gives you a commanding lead – not acquiring market share through buying and overpaying for companies. That model pulls everything together and it all starts with the five steps.'

'Yes, and it also leads to a five-level "value" test that you can use on any company.'

'What is it?'

'You know it already. If a business is a cash-compounding machine, what do you want to do with the cash it generates? Think of the "queue-for-cash" and this last model.'

Simon thinks for a moment then says, 'First, can the business pay all its suppliers, employees and the tax man on time?'

'Good, that's the basic *viability test.* What's next?'

'Can it pay back its debt and the interest on it?'

'Yes, and who else expects a "return"?'

'I do. Can the business pay me enough for my sacrifice – my cost-of-capital?'

'Right, and those two tests are what I call *capability tests* – is it *capable* of paying the "cost-of-capital", the *cost* managers ignore? What else do you want to find out?'

'That it can pay the "costs-of-the-future" to keep growing and strengthen its position.'

'Excellent, that's the fourth – the *sustainability test.* Will it be productive enough to sustain an acceptable rate of growth? Can it win more than one major tournament? Many guys have won one "major" golf championship. Few go on to win several. OK, what's the final test?'

'It's about the last chart I sent to Cole. Is there any cash left over after paying for growth? Does it create an economic profit?'

'Brilliant, Simon! That's the *desirability test.* If it does create an economic profit, that level of productivity will keep you investing there. You'll want to give them even more of your money because it equals or beats the best of your other choices.'

'So what does all that mean?'

'If a company answers "No" to any of those questions, it has a big productivity improvement opportunity. MDS has plenty of them. Get them to "Roam" round the business, Simon, and don't underestimate what you're doing. The doors of history swing on small hinges!'

'Thanks, Prof,' Simon says with a somewhat dazed expression.

'Oh, and one last thing, why don't you take a look at some other high-flying companies and maybe even do some analysis of Fortune 500 companies to test our theory?'

'OK,' Simon says. All he had wanted was a job, for Pete's sake, and now here he is rocking around the corridors of power and business academia, all because he used a simple tool that can be made available to every person in every company ... if they only knew it.

The Five-level 'VOF' Test

	Yes	No
1. **Viability:** Can you pay all suppliers and employees on time?		
2. **Capability (1):** Can you service interest and debt repayments?		
3. **Capability (2):** Can you pay the shareholders a return that pays for the 'sacrifice' they made to put cash into the business?		
4. **Sustainability:** Are you productive enough to pay for the 'costs-of-the-future'?		
5. **Desirability:** Is there cash left over, an 'economic profit', that keeps shareholders investing - do they find this firm to be at least as good as their best alternative to this investment?		

If you answer 'No' to *any* of these questions, including the last, then you have big performance improvement potential.

EPILOGUE:

'The chickens come home …!'

Nothing new comes from the next meeting Simon has with Max Ford and some of his staff. They cover the same ground, but the accountants are adamant: ROAM does not apply to MDS, a 21st-century, new economy, intellect-driven company.

In May, the MDS stock price drops to $4,50. Many people 'in the know' blame the fall on a 'market downturn', and tell Simon not to worry. They also tell him not to sell his shares, as the price will definitely bounce back. He follows their advice.

In July, MDS announces a profit warning after its denial only a few months earlier. The same evening, Simon and his Dad listen to financial analysts on a radio show. These pundits review the day's business events – especially the fall of MDS stock – and wring their hands over the 'bad luck' that befalls the poor guys who built and ran such a great business. The price halves in a day and then starts a fall during the next few weeks that eventually brings its value to a low of just under $1 before it recovers slightly – about a

90% drop from its height of $9,20 at year-end.

'Oh dear, oh dear, oh dearie me, Simon. The writing's on the wall,' his Dad says, 'and the train has left the station.'

'The boat has left the dock ...'

'The pigs have flown ...'

'The cows have come home ...'

'The fat lady has sung, and ...'

'The chickens have come home to roost!' Simon finishes off ruefully. 'My shares in MDS are lower in value than when I got them!'

'Yes,' his Dad says, 'a lot of investors have burnt fingers, and now you have three views about these guys. The first is they are as pure as altar boys but unlucky with the IT market slump. The second is they are naïve chumps for buying all these companies for so much.'

'And the third?' Simon asks.

'It may be that your basic ROAM analysis of MDS is mightily irrelevant. You see, another view is that this is a story about financially creative, harum-scarum scamps who, together with the "Hot Horse Herbies", dupe innocent and trusting investors – and a lot of greedy, gullible ones too – with smoke and mirrors, and cockamamie, IT gobbledegook. That's a harsh verdict and maybe very unfair for these guys. However, if it's true, they are not the only ones to do it. Many far bigger players have done the same the world over. 'There are companies like Cisco, Nortel, Lucent, Vodafone, Marconi and now Enron,' his Dad says, 'who, as we speak, "write off" billions and billions of dollars worth of inventory and "goodwill" from hugely over-valued acquisitions on their books. There will be more to come too – AOL Time Warner and WorldCom are both disasters waiting to happen.'

'Simon,' he continues, 'we don't know the half of it, but the important thing is to explore what we all learned from this mess and Prof. James's chicken story.'

'What do you mean by saying that my ROAM analysis is irrelevant?'

'I'm not saying you are not spot-on with your analysis. You are dead right, but the drop in asset productivity is not the main issue here. Ignore the claptrap about "new economy" companies. The dean is right. Business fundamentals haven't changed for 5 000 years. These guys have been "financially creative", not productive. There is no doubt about that. They used their shares to buy companies to grow sales, profits and earnings lickety-split because bankers, accounting firms, analysts and corporate lawyers love them for it. The trouble is all the values were crazy. The important lesson is for us to understand that.'

'I see it now. The funny thing is I couldn't bring

myself to believe we could be right. Many guys with fancy degrees and successful people I meet at the golf club all laughed. You could tell they didn't really believe what I was saying. I should have sold these shares.'

'It shows how tough it is to take the right decisions – to trust your swing under pressure. Now you'll be more confident. As I said when we started this project, very few managers know about ROAM. Even fewer use it. You do know about it. Now you must use it.'

'So are you saying that ROAM still applies?'

'Absolutely, but a big lesson for me is that "tangible" and "intangible" assets are not useful concepts any more. Why is a trademark, brand, or patent grant any less tangible than cash in the bank, an invoice, or for that matter, a robotic welder or an office building? As you said a while ago, Simon, they all exist to generate sales revenue. That's the issue.'

'So ROAM is still valid for any business, even with its limitations?'

'If it's good enough for Wal-Mart, who say they use a measure that their one million three hundred and eighty-three thousand employees world-wide can understand, that's good enough for us and anyone else.'

'So what should MDS do now?'

'Take the five steps. Before it embarked on its

acquisition strategy, especially the international one, MDS's asset base was flexible and responsive. They have to recreate that. The people who matter there know what they have to do because they have done it before.'

'How did they do it?'

'They had a simple, focussed, flexible business. Today, they have painted themselves into a corner where more than 50% of their asset base is "fixed" but "intangible". It's an apt description because there's nothing there. The guy who sold ComputeX to them cashed in his MDS shares at the earliest opportunity, and now sits on a pile of money that's burning a hole in his pocket. He doesn't know where to put it.'

'So he walked away with the value?'

'Yes, and MDS shareholders got nothing in return. There never was any value.'

'So what must they do?'

'They have a serious hangover. They spent too much time at the nineteenth hole after their golf game. Now they need a big dose of *asset spin*, and an ice-cold bath to write off all the goodwill that isn't there. In fact, the only operation that makes respectable returns is their home base. All their global ventures, the ones that account for the "goodwill", must make a lousy ROAM, but check it out.'

'I'll do it now,' Simon says. After a few

moments, he says, 'It isn't lousy, it's almost non-existent. It's about 2%. Their business model is a disaster.'

'Yes, it will lead to a massive destruction of value. Whatever happens, it'll be a very long time before they claw back the lost ground, if they ever can. That's King Cole's new challenge. He's in deep, deep rough in the woods and running out of holes to play.'

'It'll be interesting to see what he has to say when he announces their results,' Simon says.

A year later, almost exactly to the day, he studies an MDS 2001 report that has a mosaic of tiny, ghostly faces on the front cover. Pulling out his trusty calculator, he starts to hunt and peck his way through the financials. Then he updates the charts he sent to Ol' King Cole a year ago.

This is the first one – the ROS%.

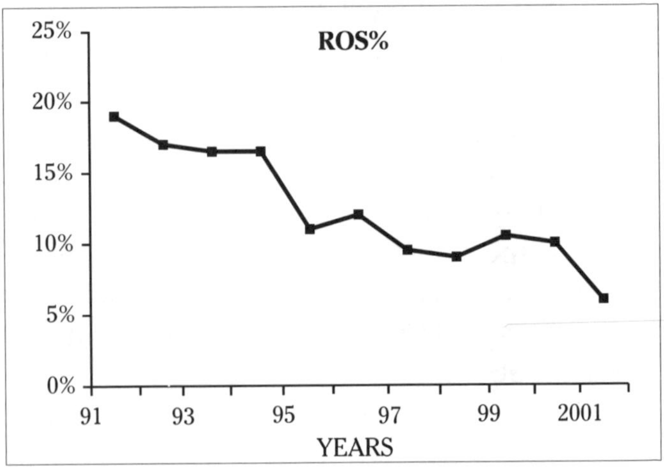

'Mmm, the low ATO climate is at work,' he thinks. 'Sales productivity plunges more than 30% from last year.'

He reads what they have to say. They blame the market conditions and axe a lot of people. Euphemistically, they call it 'counselling out of employees'.

'Oh,' he thinks, 'this "people-driven" company now has employees, not people, working there.' He wonders if the ghostly faces on the cover belong to the ones they fired. Meanwhile, top managers get a "slap on the wrist" with "no bonus", and the Board allows them to double the life of the stock options to ten years to keep them motivated.

He looks deeper into the report and finds, as he expected, that they jump into the cold bath and 'write off' $1,8 billion of shareholder value for

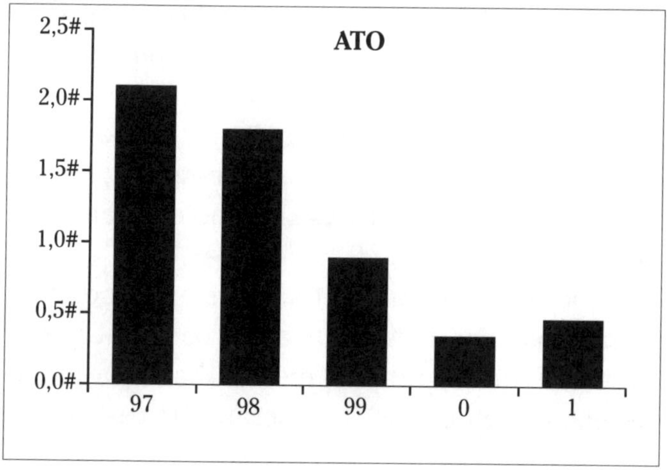

'goodwill' and other 'exceptional items'. It still doesn't make a whole lot of difference to ATO.

It is only 0,5 even after taking a huge knock. But now they focus on inventory and accounts receivable – inventory turn doubles, and customers pay 14 days sooner.

'At least they are paying attention to some basics again. Instead of driving for show, they are improving their short game at last!' Simon thinks.

'And what's this ... *ROI* ... *Return on IT Investment for customers*? That's a step forward. At least they admit returns may be important – even if they refer to customer ROI but not their own. Maybe their sales people won't be seen as "box droppers" any longer, and just *maybe* they'll start to improve customer *asset spin* as a key measure of their effectiveness.'

Then he wonders about their managers. He recalls that 'owners make a "return on investment" but *managers make a "return on assets"*. I wonder what it is now.'

'By taking a huge "write-off", the fall seems to have levelled out. It's still an accounting sleight of hand and sure destroys shareholder value,' he thinks.

He looks at the market sectors and finds that home base has 10% of the asset base but generates 40% of the EBIT. It means that 90% of the assets, the global ones, generate the rest with a

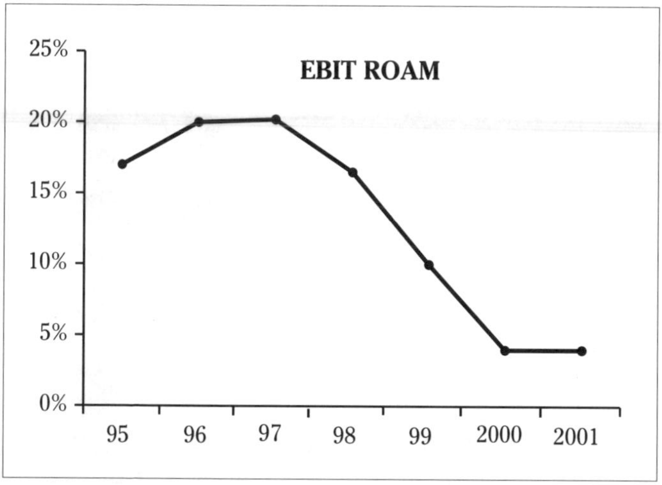

ROAM of less than 3%.

'Some business model – some global strategy! I wonder what it means for "economic profit",' Simon thinks.

He does a quick calculation, and calls out, 'Hey, Dad! Come and look at my charts.'

His father glances through them all. When he sees the last one he sighs. 'Yeah, they have a long, long haul back. The value destruction curve must be unstoppable. Some folk wonder if they have the stomach and bottle to turn it around. They've made so much money maybe they now want to enjoy it.'

Simon's next remark strikes home.

'Dad, you just said they *made* money. As a shareholder I guess they did make money for me for a while but only if I had sold my shares like

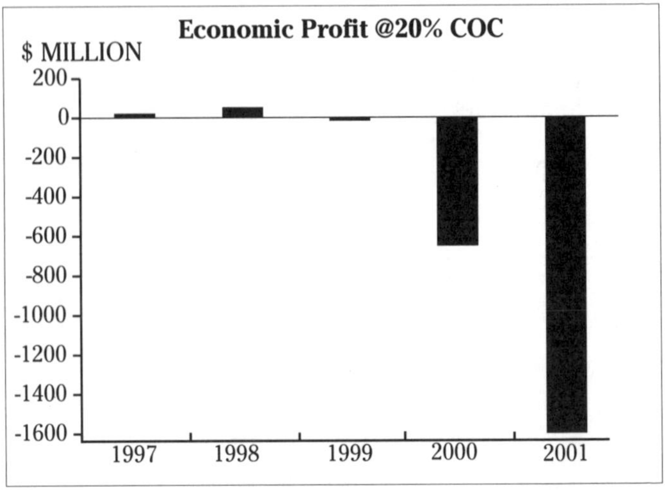

they did. After this experience, when you see what is happening to once high-flying companies around the world, if I have the chance to invest again, I shall ask: When do these managers *make* money, and when do they *take* money? *That's the question!*'

'And a very good one at that,' replies his Dad, who then gets one of those faraway looks on his face. A few moments later, he turns to Simon and says, 'How about another little project?'

Simon gives him a suspicious, sideways glance. Then he says, 'Before you tell me what you have in mind, let me show you something else.' He puts up another chart on the screen. 'I followed Prof James's suggestion and worked my way through the latest Fortune 500. I pulled out the "Average", "Best" and '"Worst" companies in

54 sectors. I had to use Profit After Tax (PAT), so I called it "After Tax ROAM" (AT ROAM). Here is a summary of the "Best".'

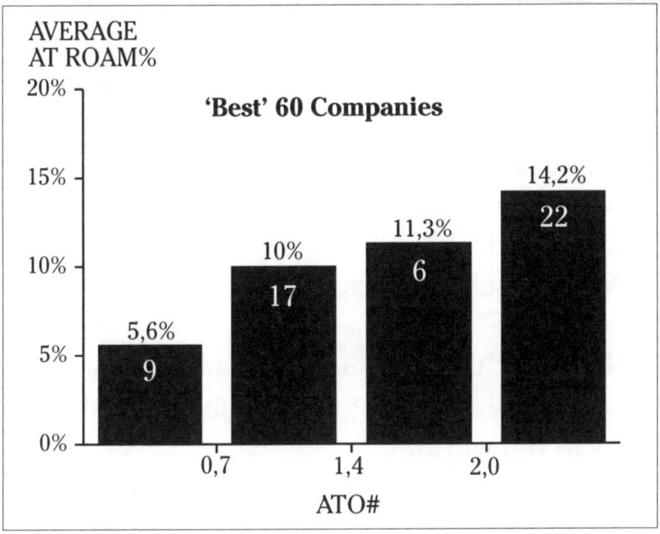

'Twenty-two companies, 4,4% of the 500, have an ATO faster than 2,0 and generate an average AT ROAM of 14,2%. An interesting ATO effect, isn't it?'

'Amazing, and it never ceases to surprise me because you always expect a black swan to come along and prove you wrong.'

'That's not all. Remember when we talked about other companies hitting white water? Well, I went on the Internet and pulled out the results of Daimler Chrysler, Cisco, Lucent, Vodafone, Marconi and Nokia. Except for Nokia, they are all doing what MDS did – winding down ATO. Nokia, on the other hand, has an ATO that is protecting it even though they are hitting some white water now. Their ATO is more than double the average of the others.'

'That's really interesting stuff Simon, and great work. Well done.'

'So, what's the next project?'

'Why don't you aim really high? Survey "The House that Jack Built".'

'Who's Jack, and what house are you talking about?'

'Jack Welch, perhaps the most admired manager in the world, built the most highly valued company in the world.'

'Which is?'

'General Electric (GE). How about testing their numbers and writing to Jack's successor? He could find he's also down in the woods today and in for a big surprise.'

'Dad! You're crazy. But then again, I thought that last time.'

He then asks, 'So are you saying it could be the "Hype, not the House, that Jack Built", just like MDS? That he binged at the same Teddy Bear's acquisition picnic that has been going on for so long now?'

'Simon, you can be the judge of that. You've become rather good at it!'

APPENDIX:

Simon's Analysis

Here are the scatter graphs he drew up from his Fortune 500 analysis. The first shows the total of 'Average', 'Best' and 'Worst' in the 54 market sectors he chose:

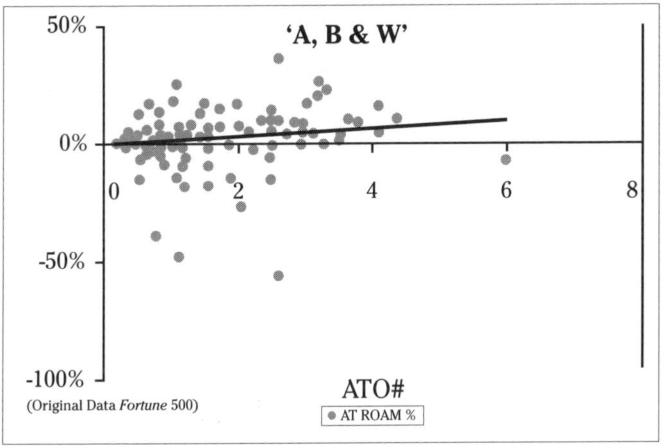

There is a positive After Tax ROAM trend line as ATO rises.

The second shows only the 'Average' companies, a more positive trend as ATO arises.

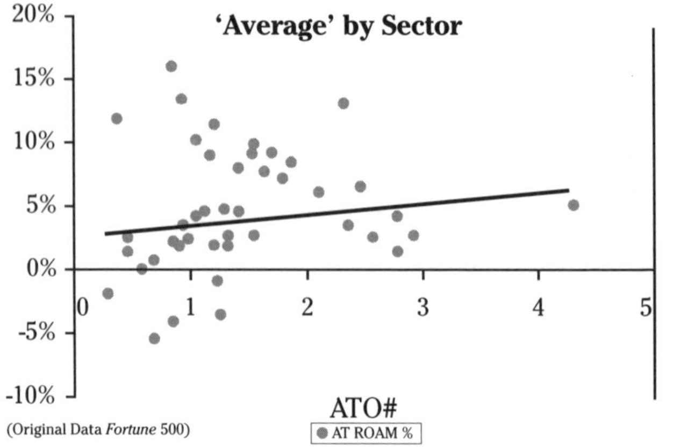

(Original Data *Fortune* 500)

Now look at the worst:

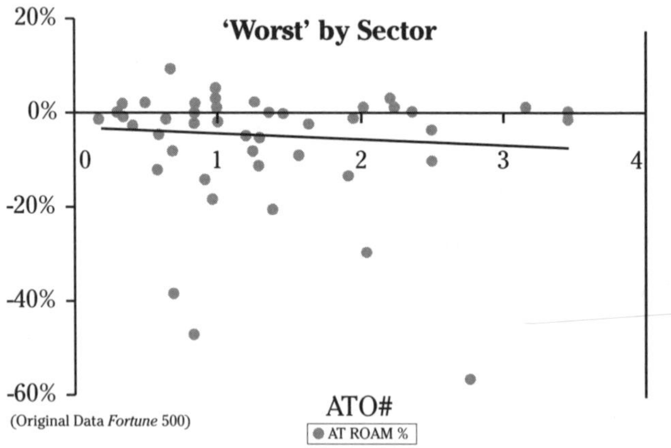

(Original Data *Fortune* 500)

The message here is that if you are losing money, pumping up the ATO will make your negative ROAM even worse!
Now look at the 'Best'! The ATO effect is clear.

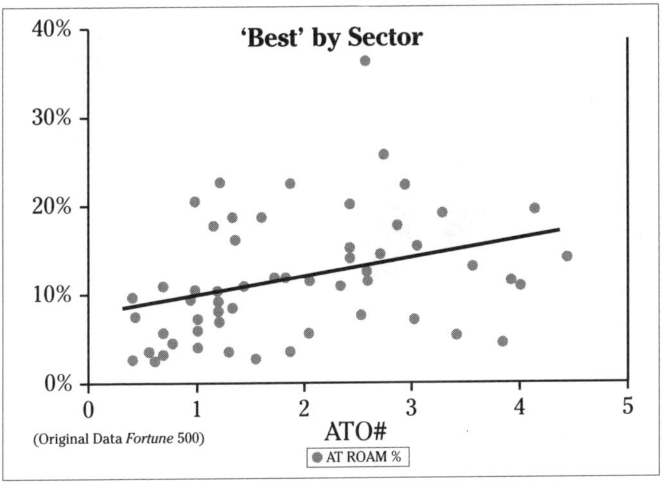

Simon also decided to look at the chicken company that Prof James talked about. He managed to go back quite a few years and found that management made an acquisition some years previously that doubled up the asset base. The effects were disastrous. The company's ROAM plummeted.

However, with redesign, ATO begins to rise sharply and so does ROAM:

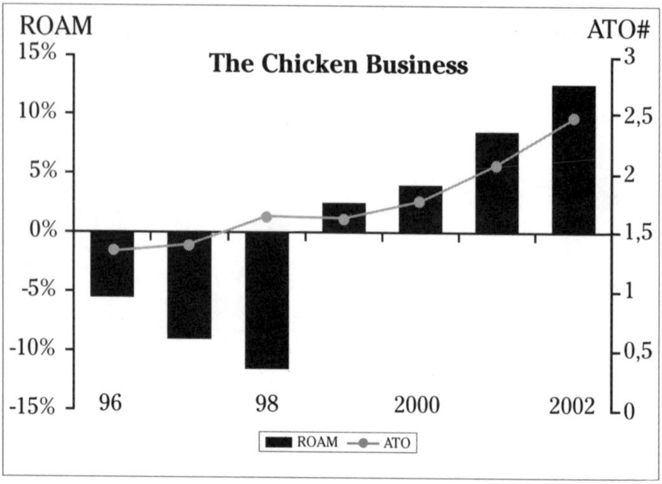

Now do the numbers for your company. You'll be in for a big surprise!

Glossary of ROAM Terms

ROAM% – Return-on-Assets Managed. It is an economic measure of productivity and expressed as a %. The resource it normally measures is the *tangible* balance sheet value of a company's asset base. However, in this story we also used the 'goodwill' that is included in MDS's balance sheet because we argue that even though it is *intangible*, it is there to create sales – just like any other asset.

ATO# – Asset Turnover. It measures the sales productivity of the asset base: 'For every $ of assets, how many $s of sales are you generating?' The answer is a number, not a % (Sales ÷ Total Assets).

Sales – This is the value of all products and/or services that a company sells during a given period. In this book, we used annual sales.

Total Assets – These are shown as *fixed* and *current* in company balance sheets. We call them *operating* and *marketing* to show who is responsible for them. *Operating* assets include all the facilities and materials used to make and get products 'ready-for-sale'. *Marketing* assets are 'finished' products and 'accounts receivable' – the cash that customers owe.

ROS% – Return-on-Sales. It measures the productivity of sales: 'For every $ of sales, how many cents profit do we make?' (EBIT ÷ Sales x 100)
EBIT – Earnings (Profit) before Interest and Tax. This is the profit number you use to calculate the ROS%.
COGS – Cost-of-Goods Sold. These are *all the costs* of getting products *ready-for-sale*. They include buying cost of materials, packaging and payroll costs as well as scrap and rework.
OPEX – Operating Expenses. These are all other expenses paid to run the business and get products and services to customers.
Value-of-the-Firm (VOF) – The number of shares in issue multiplied by the price. Two other measures used to value a company are:

- Earnings per Share (EPS) – calculated as 'Profit After Tax' (PAT) earned per share (PAT ÷ total shares issued)
- Price Earnings Ratio (PE Ratio) – the premium multiple of EPS an investor is prepared to pay for a share.

Bibliography

From First to Last (Collection of stories first published in 1947, 1948 and 1950)
Damon Runyon
Penguin Books, 1990

The PIMS Principles – Linking Strategy to Performance
Robert D Buzzell and Bradley T Gale
The Free Press, 1987

Competing Against Time
George Stalk Jr and Thomas M Hout
Simon & Schuster, 1990

Harvey Penick's Little Red Golf Book
Harvey Penick with Bud Shrake
Collins Willow, 1993

Capital Productivity: Why the US leads and why it matters
McKinsey Quarterly, 1996 Number 3

Stern Stewart's EVA – The Real Key to Creating Wealth
Al Ehrbar
John Wiley & Sons, Inc., 1998

The Profit Zone
Adrian Slywotsky
Harvard Business School Press, 1998

The Red Bead Game
John E. Black
Knowledge Resources, 1998

Fortune 500
15 April 2002

Notes

1 Page **11**: Adapted from charts contained in *The PIMS Principles* by Robert D Buzzell and Bradley T Gale – see Bibliography.

2 Page **54**: See Bibliography: *Stern Stewart's EVA – The Real Key to Creating Wealth* by Al Ehrbar.

3 Page **71**: Also adapted from a chart in *The PIMS Principles.*

4 Page **71**: See Bibliography, *Competing against Time* – Stalk & Hout.

5 Page **72**: See Bibliography, *The Profit Zone* – Adrian Slywotsky.

6 Page **77**: See Bibliography, *The Red Bead Game* – John E Black.

About the authors

Professor G S 'Andy' Andrews BCom, MBA, PhD
Andy, South Africa's leading business school academic, is a professor at Henley Management College in the UK and at IESE Business School in Barcelona, Spain.

He studied at the universities of Rhodes, Cape Town, Stanford and Harvard Business School where he completed his doctorate on the impact of corporate strategy on risk and performance. Under his leadership as Dean during the 1980s, Wits Business School at the University of the Witwatersrand, was recognised as South Africa's best.

In 1989, he started the Graduate Institute of Management and Technology, South Africa's first private business school, offering the Henley MBA programme. In 1996, he sold a major portion of this highly successful enterprise to a firm listed on the Johannesburg Stock Exchange and became deputy chairman of the holding company. He resigned in February 2000.

He has, and still serves on several boards of

directors, consults with major companies and teaches in the fields of finance and corporate strategy in South Africa, Europe and the United States. He has published over 100 articles and has received several awards for academic and teaching excellence. These include being elected as South Africa's 'Most Admired Business School Professor' on several occasions and being chosen as one of South Africa's 'Four Outstanding Young South Africans'.

Ted Black

Ted's career has taken him to the UK, Malaysia, West and South Africa. He has worked in human resources, strategic planning and organisation development. He has also gained very valuable line experience both in managing and in his capacity as a director of companies. This included some exciting years in a highly entrepreneurial and successful steel trading business.

He is now an independent consultant and author of *The Red Bead Game*, published in 1998, as well as numerous articles on productivity. He helps companies design ROAM-driven projects that turn strategy into action and develop managers, fast, furiously, measurably and productively.